The Glass Coffin,

A Reginald Sterling

Adventure

By

Charles Reeves

'… Despotism, it is their right; it is their duty, to throw off such Government, and to provide new Guards for their future security.' – Declaration of Independence

Reginald Sterling is an operative of the newly formed Office for Strategic Services. A gallant veteran of the Civil War, the War Between the States; he has been given a chance to continue to serve the new union in an organization made up of men and women working in secret utilizing the latest technology and old fashioned courage to combat America's foes. It is the new guard for the new United States. Operating outside the normal channels, the O.S.S. is investigator, prosecutor and executioner. Its operatives handle the bizarre and the unnatural seeking to guard the newly re-united states against any and all threats to its fragile stability.

It is a time of steam carriages racing beside horse drawn carts along cobblestone streets. It is a time of coal burning furnaces and people working beneath the gaslight. Gone are the gentlemen farmers that founded the American Colonies; this is the time of wealthy bankers and businessmen. It is a time of steam powered tanks, steam driven horseless carriages and mighty coal gas filled airships sailing high above the countryside. It is a time of grand adventures.

The Glass Coffin

New York City, June 1867

A lone zeppelin flies majestically across the sky over New York City, its crew looking down on the steam carriages and hundreds of people moving along the cobblestone streets. At the harbor, steam driven warships lie at anchor beside the wide wooden hulls of New England's sailing ships. Two years have passed since the end of the War Between the States and the Union has not relaxed its vigil. People still remark on the Confederate raiders that recently sailed off the New England coast. Even now, the city retains scars from the draft riots during the war. Even more recently, Brigadier General George Henry Sharpe left this harbor for Europe tasked with tracking down the last known conspirator in President Abraham Lincoln's assassination.

The U.S. Army Aero Corps zeppelin revs its steam engines pouring out eight tiny trails of black smoke as it passes over a large mansion in Manhattan. The oversized mansion dwarfs all the other buildings around it. Built with two chimneys at its center and a covered tower at each corner; it is more fort than dwelling. The zeppelin's crew looks down and sees sunlight gleaming off the brass barrel of a Gatling gun sticking out of one of the towers and a blue Union kepi being waved by a soldier from one of the other towers. The zeppelin turns lazily in the sky and heads back towards the city.

The zeppelin's crew does not question the Gatling gun or the presence of Union soldiers in the Manhattan mansion; they know well the location of the Bureau of Military Information's New York City headquarters. Formed during the War Between the States, the Bureau of Military Information, under Colonel George Henry Sharpe, provided intelligence to the Army of the Potomac and defended it from the Confederate military and its spies. Now, under Brigadier General Sharpe, the Bureau protects the fragile newly re-United States of America from enemies foreign and domestic. Expanded by Secretary of State Seward and General Ulysses S. Grant, the Bureau has grown from a fledgling intelligence service into a national security force with district offices in those states that stayed loyal to the Union throughout the long, bloody civil war.

Far below the zeppelin, on a sub level of the Victorian mansion, two young men stand stock still in their wool Union uniforms waiting their final judgment. Just as with any good intelligence service, men with combat experience and proven leadership abilities are a most valued find. Both men are veterans of the Civil War who have seen the Elephant and lived to tell the tale.

The Glass Coffin

Lieutenant Reginald Sterling looks straight ahead at the mahogany door at the end of the empty room, while the three fingered claw at the end of his steam powered clockwork left arm opens and closes unconsciously. The young man's ice cold blue eyes blink, but, his face remains blank. The twenty four year old amputee concentrates on the mahogany paneling and the room's single door while trying not to scratch the itchy wool uniform or tug on the collar buttoned tight at his neck.

Lieutenant Archibald Rawlings' lazy smile widens a bit as he hears the familiar clank of Sterling's steam powered metal hand closing. The young soldier turns his eyes to the right and sees the claw hand open and then close again with another clank and a hiss of steam. Rawlings lets his eyes wander trying to imagine what it would be like to have the small steam canisters and pistons for an arm or live each day with cold iron welded to his flesh. He stares briefly at the damp patch on Sterling's uniform where the small steam vent has soaked the wool jacket near the shoulder. Then, he snaps his eyes forward and stares at the mahogany door again; also in his mid twenties the man begins to wonder if Sasha will be at the tavern tonight. He begins to imagine how he will put the uncomfortable dress uniform to good use once the ceremony is over and he and his friend are allowed liberty for the weekend.

The mahogany door flies open and a stocky sergeant fills its frame as he walks into the room and announces, 'Attention!'

Behind the sergeant, a gray haired medium build man walks into the room and off to one side; his silver captain's bars clearly visible on the shoulders of his uniform.

'Thank you, Sergeant. Now, Misters Sterling and Rawlings, to business; I am pleased to inform both of you that as you have finished the Bureau's training with very high marks and have both served gallantly and with honor during the recent war, you will be enlisted today as Lieutenants in the Army of the Potomac. Then, as commissioned officers, you will both be transferred immediately upon enlistment to the State Department and the Bureau of Military Information's New York District posting. Are there any questions about this? Now, raise your right hands and repeat after me...'

The oath of service finished, the lieutenants salute the Captain and are saluted in return; before the captain turns an about face and walks out of the room. The stocky sergeant makes an adjustment to his immaculate uniform and smiles. Both young men look at the smile and then risk a glance at each other in warning. Sergeants do not smile unless there is something evil about to happen to someone. And Rawlings and Sterling just know they are someone today.

'Now, Lieutenants, if you will kindly follow me, I will escort you to Captain Grenville and your new assignment. While serving in Captain Grenville's unit, you will become acquainted with the aeronaut discipline and the latest in forensic sciences and field investigative methods. Now, fall in lads, time to go to work.'

'Sergeant, begging your pardon, but, shouldn't we be dismissed for liberty?' says Lieutenant Rawlings with a most unmilitary whine to his voice.

'Oh, don't you worry Rawlings, sir. There will be plenty of time later for your nocturnal deviations and pleasures, but, it would be irresponsible of the Bureau and the army as a whole to set you loose on New York society just yet. No, sir. First, we must strive to feed a little more intelligence into that starving organ you call a brain and hope that in the process you become capable of conducting yourself like a gentleman.'

'You see, sirs, you have not survived everything I could throw at you during your training here just so you can parade around in fancy uniforms. The Bureau has real work to be done. True the Rebs lost the war, but, remember those Copperhead sympathizers up in Ohio; they weren't defeated on any open battlefield, no sir. Poor President Lincoln wasn't shot on a battlefield and we still haven't gotten to the bottom of that nest of vipers and traitors. Lieutenant Rawlings, you should ask young Sterling about his Doctor Freiherr and the insanity that man cooked up before he turned tail and ran off into the night. There are still plenty of dangers to this grand Republic that need looking after and we sirs are just the men what will take care of them.'

'Sergeant, has there been word of Doctor Freiherr?' asks Lieutenant Sterling; his right arm going across his chest to grasp the warm metal of his left arm.

'No, laddie, that foul bit of insanity hasn't been seen in over a year, but, he's still out there somewhere up to no good; I'm sure of that.'

The Glass Coffin

Worchester County, July 1867

Doctor Freiherr served his country during the recent American Civil War and saved many lives with his surgeries. He envisions saving many more lives as he excises the fragile flesh of man and replaces it with iron and steam power. Unfortunately, and most unfairly to his mind, the other officers of the Army of the Potomac disagreed with his methods and his vision. He fled to avoid being locked away as a lunatic and now he must seek patronage and patients elsewhere. He knows he is on the verge of creating a new breed of man; a stronger breed of man who can withstand the rigors and the horrors of war.

So the great man of science, as he thinks of himself, finds himself in an underground laboratory beneath an isolated country estate surrounded by lush New England hardwoods. It is late in the night and outside a storm gathers; while inside the Victorian mansion's basement a strange storm of its own is brewing. A hulking brute of a man nods to the doctor before he spins a heavy brass spoked wheel turning a series of gears set along the front of a mahogany cabinet. Copper and brass rods piston out from the cabinet turning a great copper wired globe that spins with every turn of the wheel. As the clockwork gears turn the brass rods spinning a copper globe ever faster, the globe builds an electric charge and starts sending out arcs of electricity down rough copper tubing to a nearby iron framed glass walled coffin. The muscular man sheds his wool coat and loosens his tie and waistcoat before returning to the task of turning the wheel and once more the strange wire frame globe spins and sends its electricity down twisting copper tubes lighting up the inside of the iron framed glass coffin. By the electricity's sparking arcs and the dim yellow gaslight of the corner gas lamps in the basement another mystery is revealed. For the glass coffin is filled with a combination of red, yellow and blue viscous fluids and holds a floating partially clothed female body. In the dim stone basement, sparks fly as the glass coffin is electrocuted causing the fluid to boil and bubble.

Inside the glass coffin, the young woman's body jerks with electrocution. Her dark red hair floats out framing her calm face with its high cheekbones and small nose. The brute stops turning the wheel and the gears grind to a halt. The basement becomes dimmer as it is once again only lit by the gas lamps mounted on the far walls. As the sparks stop, a medium sized figure hidden beneath dark goggles, oversized rubber gloves and a black leather lab coat climbs a short ladder and reaches into the glass coffin. The mysterious man lifts his goggles and reaches into the viscous fluid of the coffin. He gently cradles the young woman's head and bends her body forward lifting her head out of the strangely warm, clinging fluids. He smiles beneath his bushy moustache and uses the rubber gloves to push the long red hair off of the woman's serene face. He takes a moment to admire the high cheek bones, small nose and calm expression on the woman's heart shaped face. With a deft motion, he peels back one eyelid to reveal a sparkling green eyeball. He grunts, and then reaches for a brass syringe from a nearby table of instruments. He cradles the woman's back with his left arm and with the other plunges the syringe into her chest and pumps its contents directly into her heart. He gently lowers her back into the fluid and climbs down from the ladder to wait.

The man beside the engine grabs hold of the wheel with both hands and turns it violently. Again the room lights up with flashing arcs of electricity and the sound of boiling fluids. The young woman sits up and screams; her emerald green eyes alive with fear. The scientist claps his gloved hands together and shouts with joy. The tall, muscular man standing in the shadows beside the machine stops turning the wheel and instinctively reaches inside his tweed waistcoat for the butt of his pistol, but, at a quick motion from the scientist reaches back to the wheel and turns it again. The woman has begun to slide back down into the fluids, but, is stopped by a third jolt of electricity and intense pain. She cries out briefly and her slender, alabaster arms fly to the sides of the coffin to hold her above the noxious fluids. The scientist lowers his dark goggles and shouts for the man in the shadows to leave the engine and come to him.

The scientist sheds his gloves and once again climbs the short ladder beside the glass coffin. He offers his hand to the woman and helps her out of the coffin. An unfamiliar, ice-like cold shoots thru her body as she steps off the ladder onto the stone floor. Her hair lies halfway down her back flowing wetly dripping rainbow riverlets of the viscous fluids. She looks around at the glass beakers, at the still glowing hot copper globe, at the hulking man walking ponderously in front of the mahogany clockwork engine and finally at the strangely attired man in front of her. She notes the scientist's cruel, dark eyes, his black greasy hair beyond the widow's peak and his fidgety hands. She squeaks a whisper of a question, asking where she is; hoping to understand the answer in such a strange place.

Instead of answering, the stranger produces a thick cotton dressing gown from a nearby table and offers it to the confused woman. She quickly wraps herself in it, suddenly aware that she is standing alone with two men dressed only in her undergarments. She feels the chill air even through the heavy cloth of the gown and her arms cling to her body seeking warmth that she no longer has. She looks round the room for a fireplace or furnace desperate to escape the icy chill that envelopes her. She focuses her frustration and fear on the man in front of her and asks again where she is and how she came to be in this dungeon.

'Dear lady, you are a guest in a friend's home. I am Doctor Heinrich Freiherr and my rather shocked, silent friend is Mr. Wilx.'

She looks around at the iron framed glass coffin and takes a step away from it shivering with dread. She looks around the room again hoping to see someone or some thing familiar to her. A young lady of good solid breeding and New England sensibilities, she is quite dismayed and frightened by her present circumstances. She stares uncomprehending at the pair of men and tries to understand the strange devilment that has befallen her.

'Do you remember your name?' Doctor Freiherr's false smile vanishes and a look of true concern shadows his weathered face.

The young lady's face grows more confused and she closes her eyes to concentrate before uttering a single word, 'Persephone'.

'Very good, your name was Persephone. Persephone Blackstone as I understand it; very good, indeed all things considered.' Doctor Freiherr says. Smiling, the scientist removes his leather lab coat and throws it unceremoniously onto a nearby table before continuing.

'Mr. Wilx, please bring young Constance into the lab. I have a feeling she'll be needed soon.'

'Now, Persephone, What is the last thing you remember?' Again, the doctor's face takes on a look of true concern for his strange patient.

Her voice sounds oddly hoarse and strained as Persephone recalls, 'I remember my parents; I live, that is we live in Blackstone Village. I remember my Thomas and Sarah Smythe. I can't remember anything else.'

'Yes, to be expected I suppose. After all you have had quite the adventure I should imagine' says the doctor.

'Sir, not to be rude, but, I don't remember meeting you. Why would my parents or Thomas abandon me to such a foul place without a proper chaperone with men I am sure I have not met?' says Persephone.

The Glass Coffin

'Ah, yes. It was fortunate for us both that a friend of Mr. Wilx's from your village was kind enough to leave you in my care, after a fashion. I am afraid your family and friends consider you quite beyond their caring now. From what the graveyard man that brought you here told me you suffered a most tragic accident. Do not fret now. It will all become clearer with time. For now, you have had quite the shock and I do believe you could do with a bit of rest' says Doctor Freiherr reassuringly.

Persephone looks down at the riverlets of red, blue, yellow running down her legs beneath the gown to form a sickly green puddle at her feet and back up at the scientist, nodding her head slowly. She does feel cold and fatigued. Rest does sound very appealing at the moment.

It is at this moment that Mr. Wilx enters the room leading a young woman wearing a long black gown with a wide white apron and a ruffled white cap into the laboratory. The young servant girl wastes no time in crossing the room and grabbing hold of Persephone's limp arm; then she leads the unresisting woman out of the room. The dark haired, pug nosed maid speaks not a word, but, leads the stumbling red headed woman, not much older than herself, to a nearby room. Constance gently helps Persephone climb beneath the heavy quilts of a four poster bed. Persephone falls asleep almost as soon as she hits the sheets. The young maid frowns as she walks out of the room; locking the door behind her; she climbs the stairs to the mansion's main floor wondering how the strange young woman came to be in the mansion and what new deviltry is stirring thanks to her employer's sinister house guest.

The Glass Coffin

The Estate of Colonel Jones, ret. July 1867

Deep beneath an isolated New England mansion, in a windowless room, a young woman with dark red hair and deep green eyes relives the last day of her life in her dreams.

Persephone looks out the side of the horse drawn carriage and remarks to her parents that it looks as if all of Blackstone Village has turned out for the clam boil and barbecue being held on the shore of the Blackstone River Canal in the lush New England countryside. She stares out at the tall wide oak trees still full of their leaves and the clear blue sky overhead. Further down the country road, women have already begun to lay out food on brand new picnic tables and men are talking of the textile mills while smoking their pungent cigars. Here and there servants busily fuss about the boiling pots of water dropping in mesh bags of clams, potatoes, onions and sausages. Further away the women pour glasses of sugar sweetened cranberry juice made locally and walk amongst the growing crowd dispensing the refreshing drinks to anyone and everyone. Persephone smiles as she catches sight of couples rowing on the calm river waters; already anxious to sneak a little privacy away from their parents. She opens the carriage door the minute the horses stop and leaps most unladylike to the plush grassy ground. She hears her father's 'harumph' followed by her mother's 'Henry, she is a young lady let her have her fun'.

Persephone raises her skirt a little and begins to thread her way thru the crowd anxious to find her suitor, Thomas. She slows and nods respectfully to the veterans of the War Between the States; poor men sitting quietly with their empty sleeves pinned up or hanging on crutches like legless scarecrows in the fields; all victims of the war and its cruel battle field medicine amputations. She briefly wonders what these men talk about as they seem to always stay to themselves. Then, she spies Thomas. She blinks and a rage begins to well up in her as a couple walking in front of her moves to the side revealing a raven haired young lady standing close to Thomas in a dress that reveals far too much for Persephone's tastes. Thomas stands gawking and talking to the young nineteen year old Sarah Smythe while she giggles and tries, no doubt, to entice him away from his courtship with Persephone.

Being the same age and having known the young Sarah since grade school, Persephone has no trouble deducing the intent of Sarah's conversation with Thomas. Persephone's green eyes glow brighter and her red hair falls out of her bonnet as she walks faster towards the couple eager to break up their conversation. Other young men and women seeing her expression step backwards or suddenly stop to let the woman pass.

Thomas feels a distinctly eerie feeling on the back of his neck beneath his sandy shoulder length hair and turns his head. His brown eyes grow wide at the sight of Persephone marching towards him. For a brief second he flashes back to the charge of the Georgians at Gettysburg, but, their eyes were not so filled with hate though the danger, he thinks, was just as real. Quickly, he turns and says his goodbyes to Sarah and steps towards Persephone in an effort to diffuse the situation. Behind him, Sarah sees Persephone and decides to melt into the crowd standing beneath a large oak tree nearby singing and clapping their hands in time with the music.

Thomas greets Persephone and pulls her close to him throwing her off balance. The young woman quickly recovers and breaks his embrace. She looks past him for Sarah, but, she is gone into the crowd. Persephone demands an explanation and instead; Thomas invites her to take a stroll along the river. Persephone is silent at first as the couple walks down to the shore to a small boat dock. Thomas hops aboard a small rowboat and invites Persephone to accompany him still hoping to distract her.

Once out on the quiet river, Persephone quickly remembers why she was angry with the fair haired muscular young man. In spite of his brief service with the Union in its valiant struggle, she cannot allow his dalliance with Sarah to go unmentioned.

Thomas sits quietly as Persephone berates him for his flirtations with Sarah. He tries to look downcast and not think about Sarah's full, red lips or her freckled bosom. He tries instead to remember why he is courting this fiery red head with her witch green eyes and sharp tongue. Why, he wonders, did he not court Sarah? He thinks of Sarah with her hearty laugh and mischievous grin so full of promise. He was so beguiled last night by Sarah's beauty, with her buxom figure and womanly charms; Sarah: who did not feel it necessary to wait for their wedding night to offer him those same charms. Thomas snaps back to the present and looks up at a particularly harsh accusation from his intended and rashly stands up in the small boat.

Persephone fears she has gone too far. She does not like the angry look on Thomas' face as he stands up in the boat and tosses the oar onto the boat's bottom with a foul curse. She hastily jumps to her feet. Thomas raises one meaty fist and Persephone tries to take a step backwards, terrified by the look of rage on his face. The small boat rocks and suddenly, she falls into the river. She tries desperately to stay afloat in her heavy dress and undergarments.

Thomas gasps. He kneels down in the boat and reaches out to Persephone in the water. His large hand touches her head beneath the waters. He tries to grab hold of some portion of her to pull her back up when a most evil and dark side of him takes control. Instead of raising her up to the boat; Thomas' hand grabs hold of Persephone's head and holds it firmly beneath the waters. His wide eyes cast around him looking for witnesses. He finds none; no one to see his evil.

Persephone grasps desperately for the boards of the side of the boat in front of her, but, can not get a firm grip. She tries to raise her head above the water, but, something holds it firmly in place. She looks to the side and can see sunlight filtering thru the water above her. She sees a lost parasol floating jellyfish like on top of the water, its handle dragging beneath the surface, much like herself. She feels her legs kicking desperately, yet, she does not rise any closer to the surface. Her day gown, never light, drags at her with the weight of the water. She wishes she had forgone the restricting corset or undergarments, but, how was she to know she would be under the pleasant river's slow moving waters and not merely sitting in the boat. She begins to feel light headed and her vision dims, still the pressure atop her head does not let up. She thrashes wildly with her arms and evokes a swift reaction when the hand pulls her head forward giving her a quick thumping against the boat. Surely, someone will see her efforts and haul her back into the warm sunlight. There is someone who should have felt her hit the side of the boat, but, she cannot remember who. Oh, where is he? She lets the thought drift away even as her lungs cry out for oxygen. She tries to duck her head and then raise it fiercely, but, to no avail; something holds her with a grip of iron. She begins to blackout and opens her mouth and takes a deep breath. The stinging cool river water floods her oxygen starved lungs and sharp pain races through her chest and then is gone; as is she. She doesn't feel the man's strong arms as they pull her lifeless body up into the warm sunlight and finally back into the boat.

Colonel Jones' Mansion. July 1867

Persephone awakes with a scream and looks around her at a stranger's unfamiliar bedroom. She eyes the gray stone walls with apprehension and looks around at the room's few furnishings. An ornately carved walnut dressing table seems out of place in such a dreary, windowless room. The dresser's mirror mocks Persephone and its many drawers and ceramic knobs open only to emptiness. Even the dressing table's carved roses seem lifeless and dull against the rest of the room. Her green eyes grow a little wide with pleasure at the sight of a beautiful russet red gown with petticoat and black corset hanging on a dressing manikin next to the dressing table. She sits up and is worming her way off of the large bed when the large oak door opens and young Constance enters the room carrying glass of something on a silver tray. The teenage servant girl puts down the tray on a small table and immediately falls into assisting Persephone dress properly in the many layers of clothing that end with the heavy rust red gown.

Persephone sits at the dressing table while Constance helps her arrange her long, dark red into a suitable chignon on her head. Persephone stands and fidgets with the fit of the corset until the servant girl hands her a long fluted glass full of red, thick liquid. A medicinal draft, the young maid explains. Persephone drinks deeply tasting a copper salty flavor she is unfamiliar with as she feels a slow warmth flow through her body electrifying her and bringing her fully awake. Persephone's eyes widen and the room seems brighter than before she drank. She cocks her head to one side and listens to the crackling of the fire in the fireplace and to Constance's breathing. In an instant, the spell of sleep is broken and she remembers where she is. Not at home with her parents, but, in a dungeon like bedroom alone and forsaken. Instead of screaming and demanding to be set free, though she dearly wants to, Persephone smiles and turns to the youthful maid and asks if Doctor Freiherr is in residence and if so would Constance be so kind as to take her to him. Constance looks into the strange woman's eyes and squeaks a yes and nods before leading her out into the hallway and down to another dark, heavy oak door. The young maid knocks hesitantly, and then opens the door in answer to a man's muffled voice inviting them to enter.

Persephone enters and looks longingly at the piano in the corner. She remembers bygone days standing around a similar cherry wood piano; her mother playing Christmas music while a younger Persephone and her bearded, distinguished looking father sing Christmas carols. How she wishes she could see her parents now; that they would show up and take her away from this waking nightmare.

Doctor Freiherr sits drinking coffee beside another heavier middle aged gentleman in the large Drawing Room. Both men stand as Persephone enters the room. Doctor Freiherr invites Persephone to sit in one of the rooms many overstuffed high back chairs. He introduces the salt and pepper haired older gentleman as Colonel Mathias Jones, Grand Army of the Potomac, retired. Doctor Freiherr elaborates that it is Colonel Jones who owns the mansion and the estate it sits on. Persephone takes a long look at the colonel. She takes in his gray mutton chops, bushy moustache and cruel thin lipped mouth before deciding she does not like him; not one bit. In spite of her bewildering circumstance, Persephone remembers to play her part and remain civil. She thanks the stranger for his hospitality, but, she is quick to ask what the gentlemen's intentions are towards her. The young Persephone stands uncomfortable beneath both men's stares; she still does not know by what means she was brought to the house, but, is sure that her parents will be worried at her continued absence. She thinks briefly of the dream and Thomas, but, surely that is not what happened. She is suddenly alarmed at the laughter from Colonel Jones when she mentions his intentions towards her and more apprehensive that neither man has made a move to enlighten her.

'As I said, Colonel, her powers of perception and reasoning have in no way been impaired by recent events; tragic as they may be. The experiment is an unqualified success. I can only deduce that the elixir sold to me by the Transylvanian chemist is indeed what he claimed and that it has healed all injuries due to Miss Blackstone's previous encounter with the Grim Reaper himself.'

Doctor Freiherr walks to a well stocked liquor cabinet and pours two tumblers of whiskey. The scientist raises one glass to his lips and holds out the other towards his host. Colonel Jones unfolds himself from the claw footed overstuffed chair and walks stiffly with the use of his cane to the cabinet and takes the proffered glass from Doctor Freiherr. He pauses to take a sip of the fiery whiskey before addressing Doctor Freiherr while openly staring at Persephone in her dress and laced boots.

'Impressive, Doctor. She does indeed appear to be in perfect health; mentally as well as physically. 'The colonel turns his cold grey eyes onto Doctor Freiherr and absently rubs his right knee as he finishes the question. 'Heinrich, old man, could this miraculous processes of yours revive its recipient cured of ancient ills as well as recent ones?'

'What are both of you prattling on about? I demand to be treated with some courtesy! You will explain yourselves at once! Why am I being held here?' Persephone exclaims. She feels oddly invigorated at the looks of alarm on the men's faces as she flies out of the chair and onto her feet in an instant. She takes one quick step forward towards the pair when Colonel Jones puts up a hand and waves her back to her chair.

'My dear Miss Blackstone; you are not being held anywhere technically. I am afraid that the time has come to explain exactly under what circumstances young Thomas brought you to shore on that most fateful and for me fortuitous day. Perhaps the good Doctor is a bit squeamish, but, I am not. You, dear woman, were the victim of a most unfortunate drowning accident while boating on the river with your intended suitor. A fact kept from you by your death and subsequent removal to this mansion wherein Doctor Freiherr and his manservant have done you the great honor of allowing you to participate in an historic experiment that has yielded you a second chance, but, at the cost of your freedom .' Colonel Jones looks from the young lady's sad, confused face to the two men looking shame faced in the corner and shakes his head.

Persephone turns away from the two men in confusion and panic and sits heavily on a red velvet couch with grotesquely huge claw feet sitting along the nearest wall. She begins to feel faint as Colonel Jones' cruel words sink in. The dress rustles loudly in her ears as she lies down on the couch while the room spins around her. Images of Thomas' angry face flash thru her confused mind. She sees a floating parasol in murky waters in her mind, while she watches Doctor Freiherr speak quietly to the suddenly appearing Mr. Wilx; no doubt summoning the maid, Constance to collect her.

Constance does indeed re-enter the room and skulks reluctantly over to where Persephone lies in the middle of the couch cradling her head in her delicate, ivory hands. Mr. Wilx walks calmly over to Doctor Freiherr and Colonel Jones. The three men converse quietly as the young maid helps Persephone to her feet and begins to remove her back to the bedroom.

The images of her watery death stop flashing thru Persephone's mind with Constance's first touch of her arm. The room settles down and stops spinning. Being manhandled is not something a Blackstone woman has to endure from any servant. With a growl, Persephone pushes Constance the maid away from her. She lurches across the room intent on grabbing Doctor Freiherr and forcing him take her home. Instead, she is met by Mr. Wilx's strong arms. She loses her balance and falls, but, quickly kicks the legs out from under nearby Colonel Jones causing him to fall heavily. Doctor Freiherr takes a step backwards and looks on in wonder at the young woman's strength and speed. Just as the young woman is standing up and demanding her release, Mr. Wilx produces a slim silver collar and snaps it around her neck. Persephone instantly tries to pull the collar off; her mind ablaze with pain and thousands of tiny red hot needles burning her neck. The hulking manservant Wilx wraps his arms around her struggling form and half carries and half drags her from the room. Young Constance quietly rushes past the pair to open the door into the hallway.

Doctor Freiherr pours himself another whiskey. He looks down at Colonel Jones and bends over offering the prostate man his hand. The colonel waves away the offer of assistance.

'If the Army had not been so stubborn and short sighted, I might have made this remarkable breakthrough during the war. Imagine, Colonel, how many needless amputations and the hundreds of young men who needn't have suffered or died. Oh, the endless hours of surgery that could have been avoided. I dare say this process could have allowed our brave men in blue to fight on in spite of any injury. Just look at the remarkable Miss Blackstone's strength and agility; her mental faculties whole and hale. A truly amazing specimen and a brilliant success for the elixir and the procedure' he remarks calmly.

Colonel Jones stands awkwardly, grabs another tumbler and pours a healthy dose of whiskey before asking interrupting the doctor's thoughts and demanding to know what in the blue blazes just occurred. The Doctor smiles as he replies that the collar Mr. Wilx so expertly placed onto Persephone is forged of the purest silver. That particular semi-precious metal being something of a bane to anyone infected with the elixir that flows thru Persephone's reanimated blood stream. He sips his whiskey and explains that the effect was purely theoretical when the Transylvanian chemist told him about it, but, it does appear to be true. Amazing, considering he only bought the necklace as a favor to the chemist; he never imagined it would actually be necessary.

Soon, there is a knock at the door and Mr. Wilx enters the room holding his arm. Mr. Wilx looks embarrassed as he explains that while she is indeed slower and weaker, Persephone can still be a danger to others; even with the silver collar on her.

Persephone's Bedroom, July 1867

The next nightfall, Persephone awakes to a terrible hunger. Her hands jump to her throat, but, the collar is thankfully missing. She sits up in the bed and tries to make sense of the events of last night. Her mind reels from what she knows to be true; that she died at Thomas' hands and somehow has been revived by the evil doctor. Persephone drops her head to her chest, but, can not cry. Instead, a foul, hatred begins to burn in her cold heart.

Young Constance has but to enter the room and Persephone jumps out of bed and glides across the room to take the fluted glass with its invigorating fluid from the girl. Persephone's long red hair falls away from her pale face as she holds her head up and drinks deeply until the bloody concoction is gone. Again, the young woman's body glows from within with deep spreading warmth and her senses come sharply alive. She is eager to let the maid help her adjust the russet gown that she has apparently slept in. Already a plan is forming in her mind and the young woman is determined that this time she will win her freedom before the strange men use some new form of torture to subdue her. Persephone and Constance walk out of the bedroom, but, it is Persephone in her swirling russet gown that leads the way to the Drawing Room.

The Glass Coffin

With a quick knock, Persephone bursts into the Drawing Room and sees Colonel Jones sitting in the far corner sitting comfortably while Mr. Wilx stands at the fireplace stoking the fire. She scans the room in one fluid motion noticing that Doctor Freiherr is not in attendance this time. Still feeling the elixir's effects, Persephone wastes no time in idle small talk, but, turns on Colonel Jones and demands she be taken home at once. The aristocratic veteran officer is at a loss for words and stammers out that she can not go home or anywhere else for that matter; given her unique condition. The colonel motions for Mr. Wilx to come closer to him; eager to have the protection of the formidable large manservant. He puts his hands on the wide armrests and thrusts downward trying to break the chair's enveloping grip. The old gentleman realizes the danger he faces as he looks at Persephone's stern face and sees the hatred burning brightly in her eyes. The colonel quickly promises to protect and care for the young woman while she is at his house, but, states that he can not give in to her demands that she be sent home. Colonel Jones leans uncomfortably on his cane and wishes he could sit back down in his red velvet high, rounded back chair. Mr. Wilx hasn't taken a step towards him and he feels far too vulnerable and alone facing the young woman's anger.

Without another word, Persephone launches herself at the older gentleman. She ducks a round house punch by the now moving Mr. Wilx and punches him soundly in the stomach in return. Mr. Wilx's dark eyes go wide with shock as the woman's slender fist doubles him over and he falls to the floor in pain. Persephone feels a sharp stab in her side and looks down to see Colonel Jones' cane, now a slim sword blade sticking thru her dress. She feels the cold blood running out of the wound and then feels it stop instantly as she pulls the sword by its blade out of her side. She twists the blade in her hand and the cane's handle flies out of Colonel Jones' hand. Enraged, Persephone throws the sword cane violently against the far wall. She looks down at the blood on her hand and time slows down. She watches in horror as her arms pull Colonel Jones to her and hold him tightly. Intense pain fills her face as pearl white fangs form in her mouth. Again, some unknown compulsion forces her head to bend forward and sink her fangs deep into the old colonel's neck. All pain is gone as she drinks deeply of the warm blood that gushes forth. A flood of new sensations fills her with strength and warmth. She is filled with a pleasant tingling sensation flowing all thru her body. Her mouth is alive with the salty, coppery taste of the man's blood. The strength flowing into her limbs is a thousand times better than the pale imitation found in Sarah's cold elixir. She holds the old man tightly as a lover would and drinks until no more blood gushes forth; then, throws his empty corpse into his chair. She turns suddenly, her body and mind alive and flooded with warmth and strength. Mr. Wilx looks up from the floor and then folds his arms over his face in fear. Persephone looks at Sarah, but, she too is cowering and trying to hide from her sight.

Persephone throws open the door and runs down the hallway. She sees a stairway on her right hand side and flies up the stairs to the house's main floor. Hardly pausing to grab hold of the doorknob, the young redhead flies out the front door and into a moonlit night. She glances around, but, sees and hears no one. She looks around the cobblestone courtyard at the building joined to the multi-gabled mansion and at the barn on the far side of the courtyard. Her eyes narrow as she searches for an exit and sees only the rough stones of a wall running around the courtyard's border. Then, her gaze falls on a stone archway open beneath the night sky. She runs across the courtyard and out the arch to freedom. Stands of tall pine trees fill the landscape on either side of a single lonesome dirt road. The young woman brushes away her loose hair, black beneath the moonlight and raises glowing green eyes to the full moon above. She watches as a lone airship glides silently thru a black sea of sky and silently makes its way across the milky white moon. She tries desperately to think of her next move while watching the tiny propellers twirl and push the great airship towards some far off land. 'Thomas!' she says and then repeats the name with a throaty growl and an evil smile. She dashes off across the road and deep into the woods.

Persephone looks up thru the tree limbs trying to catch a glimpse of the mysterious airship. Her dress tangles on the underbrush and she pulls it free with a tearing noise and trudges deeper into the forest. She has only one thought; home and a reunion with the traitorous Thomas. She has no clue what her new life will be like or what will ultimately become of her, but, she knows that she must repay Thomas for his treachery. So she walks thru the forest beneath the dim light of the moon overhead; her unique condition giving her eyesight a noticeable boost and keeping her steps steady and swift.

The Glass Coffin

Doctor Freiherr's Laboratory, July 1867

Back in the lowest level of the mansion, Doctor
Freiherr exits the laboratory amidst the sounds of
Persephone running up the staircase at the end of the
hallway. He takes off his gloves and goggles while he
walks slowly towards the Drawing Room; anxious that he
is late, but, enthusiastic about his latest experiment's
success. His hand is just touching the doorknob to the
sitting room when the door is flung open from the inside
and Mr. Wilx suddenly fills the doorway; almost knocking
the older scientist off his feet. Doctor Freiherr takes one
look at his manservant's distressed facial expression and
demands to know what has happened. Mr. Wilx steps back
and points with a muscular arm ending in a hairy knuckled
huge hand at the slumped body of Colonel Jones slumped
lifelessly in his high back chair. Damnation, swears Doctor
Freiherr. He quickly examines the dead man and motions
for Mr. Wilx to come to him. The muscular servant and the
doctor lift the lifeless body and carry it out of the room.
Moving as fast as they can in an awkward step shuffle, the
pair move down the hall into the laboratory; slamming the
door behind them.

Quietly, slowly, Constance lifts herself off the floor
from behind another of the overstuffed chairs and makes

her way into the hallway. She immediately takes off following in Persephone's footsteps and flees the house. She pauses upstairs only long enough to empty the contents a wood and ivory inlaid box containing household monies for groceries and such. She dare not even go to the top floor and retrieve her meager belongings from her room. No, she thinks, there is nothing among her possessions that would necessitate another moment alone in the strange mansion. She runs outside and immediately turns onto the dirt road eager to escape the mansion and its horrors.

In the laboratory, Doctor Freiherr hastily refills the glass coffin with its noxious mixture of chemicals and fluids; all hard pressed to acquire and impossible to replace. He looks over at the shaken Mr. Wilx and smiles humorlessly. A bad night all around for everyone, he thinks. At least, Colonel Jones will have his turn in the experiment as he wished; just a little sooner than expected. A shame about Persephone, he would have liked to study her for a bit longer; but, like her namesake she is gone from death's lands and once more free to roam amongst the living.

'Mr. Wilx, tonight we shall learn if my process can heal was well as resurrect. I am concerned that the Colonel's injuries will prove too extensive for a complete recovery, but, science must advance and I am sure the colonel would want us to proceed. Kindly activate the electro-magnetic engine, if you please and let us tend to our benefactor', says Doctor Freiherr finishing with a nasty smile. The scientist pulls on his tinted goggles and gloves and stands back, rubbing his hands together unconsciously.

Mr. Wilx shakes his head as he removes his jacket and waist coat before grabbing the brass spoked wheel and giving it a vicious turn. He spins the wheel with all the force of his penned up rage at losing Persephone and allowing the colonel to come to such an end; even if it is temporary. He turns his head and watches the electricity arc to the glass coffin and sees the fluids boiling around the colonel's lifeless body. He winces as the doctor climbs the steps of the short ladder carrying the large brass syringe and stabs the body in the chest releasing the last of the Transylvanian elixir.

A few minutes later, Colonel Jones' scream resonates through the laboratory announcing the experiment's success.

A New Plan Unveiled

A few days later at the mansion's underground level and a newly arrived young maid in a long black gown wearing a wide white apron with her black hair hidden beneath a white cap walks over to Colonel Jones as he sits in his customary chair smoking a cigar. The young maid hands her master a tall glass of dark red liquid and quickly turns away from the look of avarice in his eyes. Across the room, Doctor Freiherr sips his whiskey and tries not to stare at his patient's greedy guzzling of the medicinal draught. He instead concentrates on the slender youthful body of the domestic as she twirls away and exits the Drawing Room. Mr. Wilx enters the room loaded down with rolled maps and a stack of hand written papers. The burly man walks to a wide mahogany coffee table and spreading his arms wide, dropping everything on the table's marble inlaid surface. He bends over the table trying to capture the rolling maps and re-order the papers. A smiling Doctor Freiherr starts walking to his assistant, but, is stopped by Colonel Jones' next comment.

'Doctor Freiherr my good man, what prarmored personnel enginess in countering the annoying side effects of your otherwise marvelous experiment?'

'There is cause to believe that the day sickness can be overcome with time. I am still working on the mathematics, but, I see no reason why we can not have you see the light of day, eventually. At the moment, I am in suffering a lack of certain compounds needed to test my theories. It would seem that when we initiated the second experiment, prematurely and unexpectedly, I used all of the material on hand. Not that I am complaining, the experiment was a success and certainly could not be delayed.'

'Glad to hear my death did not cause you too much distress. I would hate…that is I am terribly sorry that my death and re-animation has precluded you from more worthy use of the chemicals. However, this dreadful sleep disorder imposed on me by the rising of the sun is unbearable and must be reversed. What use is super human strength and vigor if it can so easily be crushed by the light of day?' Colonel Jones stands, stretches luxuriously and glides to the fireplace in one fluid motion.

'Colonel, I do understand your distress. Unfortunately, Persephone's departure came before I could properly examine her to find the cause and cure for the side effect. I will have to use what little information I can gather from blood and tissue samples for now. Oh, and may I say I am glad to see that my procedure has indeed cured your old misfortunes as it reversed your recent untimely demise. Unfortunately, in order to continue my work I will need to procure some rather esoteric compounds and rare chemicals if I am to track down a cure to the side effect you mentioned.'

'How may I be of assistance, Doctor? My resources are at your command. You have me at a rather hefty disadvantage these days. You have merely to make a list of these chemicals and send any of the house staff to town to fetch them for you. I fail to see the difficulty here. After all, had it not been for Mr. Wilx's superior handling of young Miss Blackstone, I would not now be in so desperate need of your services to escape this half life your experiment has condemned me to.'

'Colonel, please. I could not have foreseen the extremes to which the young Persephone would be driven and certainly would have taken more precautions had I known how dangerous she would turn out to be. Speaking of young Miss Blackstone, Mr. Wilx, what have you heard of our ungrateful guest since her departure?'

'It would seem her suitor Thomas has fallen victim to some wild animal attack. He was found dead in a disreputable part of town, but, the newspaper did not give many details on the condition of the body. No one has reported seeing Miss Blackstone herself in or near the town.' So saying, the big man shrugs and shakes his head slightly.

'No matter, she will eventually turn up one way or another. The pressing matter for now is the replenishment of my stock of chemicals so the next phase of experimentation can begin. Colonel, I come to you directly as the peculiar compounds and chemicals I need can not be easily had. Mr. Wilx has found a source, but, it is not commercial. It would seem that there is a large batch of just the sort needed being shipped to a nearby hospital in Millbury. Unfortunately, these supplies are not for sale, but, will need to be gotten using rather unorthodox means.'

Colonel Jones' eyes narrow as he says, 'Unorthodox, as in acquired without the owners' consent?'

'I am afraid so, Colonel. I will indeed have to burden our relationship with a request for resources, but, not money this time. Mr. Wilx has concocted a rather ingenious plan for liberating the supplies I need from the train carrying them, but, it calls for more muscle and resources than he can provide.' Doctor Freiherr replies.

'Ah, I am intrigued. I have come to think your Mr. Wilx can handle any situation. Let's do have some whisky and discuss your plan for liberating these chemicals... from a train was it.'

Colonel Jones watches, sipping his whiskey, as Mr. Wilx produces a roll of paper and flattens it out on the mahogany coffee table revealing a map of the Massachusetts countryside and the iron spider web of railroad lines that connect its towns. He watches as Doctor Freiherr walks past and helps Mr. Wilx anchor the edges of the map. The aging colonel walks slowly to the table and looks at the map and then at Mr. Wilx.

'Now, Doctor, Colonel, I have been giving this quite a bit of thought. According to an associate of mine in Fitchbury, the chemicals the doctor is anxious to procure are being shipped out Thursday on the morning train bound for a hospital in Millsbury. As I studied the railroad lines it seems to me there is a goodly stretch of empty countryside between some of the smaller stations along this route. If you look at the map, you see Oakdale is the only major rail station that the train will pass through and then there is quite a bit of rail to cover before it comes to the next station. What I propose is that a small band of riders could stop the train while it is in this empty countryside and with the use of a sturdy wagon remove the desired crates of chemicals and bring them back here. Note, gentlemen, there may be need of gunplay in convincing the railroad workers to part with their cargo.'

'A very sound plan and unexpected in its audacity. I do not believe I have ever heard or read of a train being robbed here and should be quite surprised if anyone would expect such a lowly cargo to require guarding', says the colonel with an amused expression.

'Yes, sir. That was my thoughts; it will be an unexpected gambit. Unfortunately, I do not have any qualified associates as I would trust with such an undertaking.'

'I see, now as I see it, what is needed is a small troop of trustworthy men, good with a horse and a pistol that will risk much and talk little.'

'Yes, that is exactly the sort of fellows needed.'

'Well then, Mr. Wilx, Doctor, I believe I can assist you. I have in mind some of the men who rode with me during the war. True they are a bit down on their luck these days, but, they were good soldiers and good horsemen. I shall see if I can contact them tomorrow. For now, however, I would like to discuss this plan in some details and see if we can put some more meat on this dish.'

To Block out the Sun

In his laboratory, Doctor Freiherr works intently on modifying a heavy gray cloth diving suit. He looks over the heavy leather gloves for any hole no matter how small. The diving suit like contraption needs few alterations. The doctor instead is free to concentrate on applying a polarizing film of his own invention. He paints a thin coating on the outside of the glass face plate of the brass helmet; careful to ensure no light may enter after the coating is done. He turns the diving helmet over and looks for any other pieces of clear glass and applies more coatings to them. When he is done and satisfied at the quality of the job; all of the glass is able to block out the sun's direct rays. He wonders briefly how well the colonel's new eyes will see thru the darkness.

The doctor sets the helmet aside and walks to another table and studies a boiling beaker of greenish liquid shaking his head slowly. He dips an eyedropper in the beaker and draws off a small amount of the fluid and moves down the table to a dead human arm laid out in an iron pan. He squeezes the bulb and the liquid rushes out and onto the arm's hand. The demented ex-surgeon is not sure if the fingers move minutely or if it is only his imagination and will to see them move. He simply must

The Glass Coffin

have more material for his research. The doctor is startled by a quick knock on the door and Colonel Jones quickly enters the laboratory.

'Doctor Freiherr, greetings. I have renewed my acquaintance with four very capable gentlemen with just the right temperament for your little adventure. They have been briefed as best as possible on the items we are interested in acquiring. I have instructed them to meet the 8am train out of Oakdale tomorrow morning at the site Mr. Wilx and I agreed on last night. I trust Mr. Wilx's sources are accurate and the consignment will meet your needs. I should hate to go thru the trouble and expense of this for nothing.'

'Oh, quite sufficient I am sure. Oh, as long as I have you, would you be so kind as to try on this suit; once the side effect is cured I think this will be adequate for your daytime uses should you wish to leave the mansion.' The older gentleman squirms into the suit like an eel and manages the heavy materials as another man would wear a dinner jacket. The doctor is about to ask the Colonel about the heavy brass helmet's faceplate and its dark coating when the man walks around several tables and back to the startled doctor without a single hesitant step.

Colonel Jones reaches up and takes off the heavy diver's helmet effortlessly and says, 'This plan of Mr. Wilx, it will succeed.'

Doctor Freiherr stares at the heavy brass helmet being held effortlessly by the older gentleman and nods while trying to decide if the statement was a question or a command. He looks up to Colonel Jones' face, 'Yes, but, the Transylvanian elixir has been exhausted and I have no way to replace that. I will have to alter the process or enrich the formula with an alternative in future experiments. I do not doubt Mr. Wilx's abilities to plan this adventure and I will, of course, trust that you have hired capable men to execute the plan.'

'The formula cannot be duplicated because of this Transylvanian substance? There is no way to re-animate anyone else, to make them as you have made me?'

'Temporarily, yes, I have come to the end of that road. But, you and Persephone survived and that line of experimentation has succeeded beyond my dreams. I am certain I can use the new chemicals and what I have learned to improve upon the process. I do wish we had been able to study Miss Blackstone a while longer.'

'Yes, Miss Blackstone. You do bring up an interesting point in mentioning her; she could return on her own seeking some form of twisted revenge. She thinks me dead, but, you are still here and alive.'

'I had not thought… Perhaps there is something I can do to improve security of the estate and the grounds. Now, where is my notebook? I must consuLieutenant. Oh, yes, Mr. Wilx will no doubt have an adequate map of the surroundings…'

Laughing, Colonel Jones sheds his suit and walks unnoticed out of the laboratory as Doctor Freiherr begins lighting gas burners and gathering glass beakers together on a far off table.

The Hospital Train

A steam locomotive chugs its way across the countryside trailing a black column of smoke. Inside the engine compartment, Bernie, the engineer, whistles a lively tune as he drives the steam train down its iron tracks past fields of lush green grass and wide, towering oak trees. Beside him, young James opens the furnace door with a blast of warm air and quickly shovels more coal into the fire. The lanky youth closes the furnace door with a hasty motion and tosses his shovel back onto the coal bin. The aging engineer takes off his hat and lets the cool morning wind blow thru his thinning hair. He puts his hat back on and looks over at the young stoker; the boy is busy munching on a crisp red apple. The engineer shakes his head; he's watched the boy eat more in a day than men twice his size. Youth is truly an amazing thing.

The engineer adjusts a dial studiously controlling the steam and by it the speed of the heavy steel train. The fifty year old man sighs and leans out the side of the engine compartment again. Bernie gasps and blinks his eyes in disbelief. His eyes can't believe what he is seeing. The scenic morning is ruined as he stares at a wooden wagon lying upturned across the tracks blocking the train's path. It will almost certainly derail the train if they hit it.

The Glass Coffin

Recovering from the shock, the engineer reaches up and pulls a chord creating a long shrieking whistle blow. He spins the valves and pulls the levers locking the train's brakes and blowing off steam. A cloud of steam envelopes the train engine. James holds on to the side of the compartment to keep from falling and complains about the noise; the screaming high pitched whistle and the somewhat deeper, scraping sound of metal on metal as the brakes try to slow the train. The young stoker lurches to one side and falls partway out the compartment's open window. Looking up ahead he sees the cause for Bernie's erratic actions and instantly shares the older man's fear.

The train screeches to a stop twenty feet short of the upturned wagon. Bernie continues to work frantically to bleed off the steam and bank the fire that James has maintained so well. James for his part keeps a watchful eye on the wagon making sure it doesn't come any closer. The boy suddenly turns his head and shouts for Bernie to come to his side of the compartment. Bernie fears for his heart as he gets the second shock of the morning.

The old man and the boy both climb down the engine's ladder and start waving and shouting at four horsemen riding fast towards the train. They both fall silent as the horsemen draw near and then draw six shooters. Bernie and James stare open mouthed, absently raising their arms above their heads as one of the horsemen peels away and rides up to them. The man grins thru a dirty black beard at them while the other three horsemen ride up to the baggage car behind the coal car and the now silent engine.

The three horsemen dismount and are just about to open the baggage car's wide sliding door when the car's attendant opens it for them. One of the raiders panics and shoots the man. He falls out of the baggage car onto the green grass; dead.

'Damnit Ed. What did you do that for?' Carl demands.

'Sorry, Carl. I wasn't lookin' for him to come out like that.' Ed replies.

'Well, alright. Let's get in there and do what we came to do and be gone.' Carl says.

The three men dismount and enter the baggage car. Carl runs to the back of the compartment and starts looking for the crates as described to the men by Colonel Jones. Ed and the third raider start ransacking the mail bag and anything else that looks like it might contain valuables. Their search yields a small bag of gold and silver coins and the less desirable treasury notes bound for the payroll

The Glass Coffin

department at a nearby coal mine. The two men shout and congratulate each other as Carl comes grinning down the aisle. He has found the chemical crates.

'Alright now, Ed. You and Bob here go get the wagon and let's load up.'

The two men leave the baggage car smiling and ride their horses up to the upturned wagon. The men waste no time in tying ropes to the wagon's side and walk the horses back away from it until the wagon is pulled over and back onto its wheels. Ed and Bob start to plan how they will spend their pay while hitching their horses up to the wagon.

A tired Bernie looks down the rails at the dead baggage attendant's body lying in the grass and then at the still grinning gunman in front of him. Two men on horses ride past only to return minutes later with their horses hitched to the now righted wagon. The old engineer looks on not believing his eyes as the raiders load a couple of cloth sacks and a dozen wooden crates from the baggage car into the back of the wagon. The horseman in front of James and Bernie makes a noise and points his gun at the ground repeatedly until the two of them get on their knees. Bernie and James both close their eyes and pray; preparing for their death.

'Bob, you sure we got all the crates the Colonel wanted? I don't like the idea of disappointing the old man. Sure feels good to be running for the Colonel again, almost like the good old days' says Carl.

'Yeah, Carl, what wasn't nailed down is in the wagon to be sure' says Ed.

In front of the train, the gunman waits until the wagon has rolled into the thin line of woods before turning his horse and galloping off after the other raiders. A few minutes later, Bernie risks opening his eyes; the horsemen and the wagon are gone.

The Glass Coffin

Chemicals Delivered, a Secret Revealed

The sun is moving low in the western sky when the raiders come riding into the courtyard escorting the wagonload of crates and sundries from the train. Expecting Colonel Jones, they are a little disappointed at being met by Mr. Wilx instead. He quickly explains that the colonel is off on an errand and will be joining them at dinner that night.

Mr. Wilx leads the raiders around the back of the mansion and opens a secret door built into the rear of the mansion's brick wall. The raiders carry the crates down a short flight of stone steps into a large dungeon like room lit only by the dim, yellow light of the gas lamps along its walls. As Wilx leads the men into the laboratory, his mind drifts back to the arrival of another wagon in the evening and the fateful night he carried Miss Persephone Blackstone's lifeless body into the laboratory.

The raiders pile their crates of chemicals on the stone floor and try to ignore the strange machinery and cluttered wooden tables. Ed especially tries not to see the emaciated corpse strapped to one of the tables or the arm in its glass container twitching with unnatural life. Carl sets down his crate and stares at the iron framed glass coffin that dominates the center of the macabre room. He stiffens as Mr. Wilx puts his hand on his shoulder.

'I said, if you would be so kind as to take the wagon around to the barn and have your men stable the horses, I will meet you at the front entrance and we can wait for Colonel Jones' arrival in more comfortable surroundings.'

The raiders enjoy a meal of cold mutton and a pitcher of local beer as the sun sinks beneath the horizon leaving a burning red sky to turn black with night. The raiders laugh and exaggerate their daring while giving Mr. Wilx the highlights of the train robbery. Mr. Wilx smiles a genuine smile as the raiders praise his planning, even though they credit Colonel Jones with being the mastermind for the raid. Still, the Doctor has his chemicals and no one knows where the raiders came from, small matter to him who is credited for the deed. He is about to ask Carl a question about the safe when the Dining Room's oak door slides open and Colonel Jones makes his entrance.

The colonel greets his guests and thanks them for their successful service. He frowns as Carl begins the tale of the great train robbery again and soon all the raiders are replaying their roles. Mr. Wilx sits smiling as he notices the odds increasing against success with each retelling of the robbery.

The colonel listens intently at least on the surface; while his head screams for more of the doctor's elixir and a strange desire that is building within him. Finally, he throws a fistful of the new treasury notes on the table and abruptly thanks his ex-soldiers for their services. Carl frowns until the colonel promises that he will contact them should their services be needed again. With a curt goodbye, the colonel retreats back down the stairs to a waiting goblet of blood red elixir and the solitude of the underground Sitting Room.

Mr. Wilx is left alone to see the men out the front door of the mansion and make feeble apologies for the colonel; no doubt an ailment has the better of him. Carl and the other men nod in understanding; the colonel is getting older. The raiders walk out to the stable talking amongst themselves about the robbery. Carl stops in his tracks as Ed makes the comment that the men do not need the colonel; only another wagon and a train.

Worchester County, August 1867

It is early morning a few days later and another locomotive steams innocently across the Massachusetts countryside bound for Boston. The train engineer watches his gauges and the tracks ahead while the young stoker watches the tall grass and wide oak trees, their leaves just starting to turn yellow, red and orange, as the train speeds past. Overhead, a brilliant sun peaks thru white billowy clouds floating in a blue sky. The train's wheels clank along as they roll over the iron rails. The stoker throws another shovelful of coal into the fiery furnace before going back to watching the countryside flash past.

Suddenly, the early morning calm is pierced by the shrill wail of the train's steam whistle. The engineer desperately throws levers downward and spins brass wheels closed trying to bank the fire in the furnace and engage the train's brakes. The brakes squeal loudly and sparks fly from the wheels. The iron steam engine bounces over a loose section of rail. The young stoker cries out when he sees the overturned wagon blocking the tracks up ahead. The youth tries to help the engineer stop the train. Both men lean out of the open engine compartment and watch helplessly as the wagon grows ever nearer looming larger by the second.

The Glass Coffin

The young stoker sees the horsemen galloping across the grassland towards the train. He turns back to the engineer and shouts a warning; certain that the approaching riders have something to do with the wagon and the train's distress. The engineer and the young stoker fall to the metal floor as the brakes release causing the train to shutter before bucking forwards with a sudden increase in speed. The engineer pushes himself up to his hands and knees; gripped by a horrible thought. Overheated and ill maintained; the brakes have failed.

Carl watches in disbelief as the train continues forward and collides with the overturned wagon. The raiders' leader doesn't understand why this engineer didn't stop the train in time. Instead of riding up to the engine; the raiders all rein in their horses and watch in stunned silence as the wagon explodes on impact with the great steam engine. Pieces of shattered wood and a cloud of black smoke fill the air.

'Holy Fire! Carl, did you see that? The wagon just disappeared when that train hit it' says the portly raider, Ed.

'Yeah, Ed. I think we all saw it. Carl, what do we do now? I thought sure they'd stop like the first train did. What we gonna do?' says the lanky raider Luke.

'Why didn't they stop? They had to see the wagon! Just don't make good sense' says Ed.

'Alright, so they didn't stop. Can't help that now. Let's get in there and open that baggage car and see if what they're carrying is worth losing a wagon over. Our aim is the same, don't matter if they stopped or the wagon stopped 'em. Ride for the baggage car and let's get in and get out.'

'Right, Carl.'

'Right, Boss.'

The four horsemen resume their galloping ride to the train's baggage car. The first rider dismounts just as a shaken, bloody middle aged man opens the baggage car's sliding wood door. The man wipes his bloody brow and stands ashen faced as the first raider draws his revolver and tells him to step down from the doorway.

Carl and Luke dismount and walk into the railcar, leaving Jim and Ed to watch the shaken baggage car attendant. They draw their pistols as they look around at the overturned crates and tumbled, broken boxes that litter the boxcar. The men glance towards the middle of the car and spot a black and red steel safe sitting amongst the general chaos of the car's contents. Luke steps forward towards the safe just as a man in a pinstripe suit stands up on the other side of the safe. Luke has seconds to register the cut on the man's head and the blood coursing down his forehead before the railroad agent raises his pistol and shoots Luke in the arm; shattering the bone. Luke spins around with the bullet's impact and drops to his knees. The skinny man screams and curls up upon himself.

Carl thumbs back the hammer on his pistol and fires. Black powder explodes in a tongue of flame from the octagonal barrel and a bloom of bright, red blood appears in the pinstripe jacket covering the railway man's chest. He falls backwards without a sound. Carl curses quietly as he stalks forward. Seeing the agent's glassy eyes staring lifelessly up at the ceiling, the raider turns around and calls out to Luke.

Luke's muffled answer is more painful outburst than speech, but, it is enough to reassure Carl that his friend is not dead. He watches as Luke stands up, blood flowing between the fingers of his right hand as it holds tightly to his left bicep. The man says something unintelligible to Carl before walking unsteadily out of the baggage car. From outside, Carl hears a familiar voice.

'Carl you okay? Holy ... Luke what happened to you?'

'Jim', Carl yells, 'Railroad agent shot Luke get Ed to look after him and send me that baggage attendant; he's got a safe to open up.'

Carl is watching the shaking attendant's second attempt to open the safe. The middle aged baggage man turns the safe's black iron handle and opens the door. Carl leans forward just as the sound of a shotgun blast outside fills the baggage car. Carl stands up and starts running for the open doorway. The roar of unseen pistol shots causes him to crouch and duck waddle slowly to the open doorway. He cocks the hammer of his revolver and pokes his head just outside car's wall until he can see.

'Jim, Ed! What's going on out there?' says Carl.

'Carl, some kid just shot Jim in the back with a shotgun. I think he's dead!' says Ed.

'You useless ... he's not dead, but, that boy is.' says Luke.

Carl climbs down from the baggage car's entrance and looks around him. Luke is kneeling beside a man lying face down in the grass and farther up the train near what's left of the engine compartment lies the body of the young stoker; two bloody bullet holes in his chest.

'What more can go wrong? I don't believe this. Ed, make yourself useful and get in there and clean out that

safe before the railroad man does it for himself. No, not
with your bare hands, take our saddle bags and fill 'em with
everything in that safe. God knows we earned our money
today.'

'Luke, how bad off is Ed?'

'He caught a load of buckshot in the back. He'll
live, but, he aint gonna be dancing anytime soon.'

Carl walks to the two wounded men shaking his
head the entire time. He helps bandage Luke's arm with a
bandana before the two of them hoist Jim up onto his horse.
The men tie the stricken raider to his saddle with a length
of rope and mount up themselves. Behind them, a smiling
Ed comes bounding out of the baggage car waving saddle
bags stuffed full of legal tender notes and gold coins.

The two healthy raiders ride behind their wounded
compatriots as the raiders gallop off into the woods and
away from the ill fated train. Luke curses with every
bounce of his horse as the bullet in his arm moves around
like a red hot poker. The ever quiet Jim is slumped low
over his horse making a low steady moan. The raiders
know that they need medical attention. They also know
that showing up at the hospital with two men suffering
from gunshot wounds will send all of them to jail. The
raiders' leader makes a fateful decision to ride for Colonel

Jones' mansion. It is the only path open to the men that might get Luke and Jim the medical attention they need to survive. Surely the colonel's personal physician is a capable surgeon, thinks Carl. He only hopes that they will be welcome; he hasn't quite forgotten the colonel's strange behavior or their abrupt dismissal.

Birth of the Iron Men

Doctor Freiherr is surprised to hear knocking at the laboratory's secret door along the outer wall. He pushes up his goggles and opens the heavy door. He quickly takes a step back as four men rush past him. The doctor recognizes the men as the ones that delivered his wagonload of chemicals from the train robbery the other day. He is very confused to see them in his lab; his confusion turns to alarm as he notices the blood trailing from one's arm and another man's back. What manner of trouble has befallen these men and the mansion for them to take sanctuary here, he wonders. The two healthy raiders lay their bleeding friends onto nearby tables. Carl walks over to the lab coated doctor and tries to explain Luke and Jim's injuries. Doctor Freiherr is greatly relieved when Mr. Wilx walks into the room.

The faithful manservant first talks to the leader of the raiders and then begins trying to calm down Doctor Freiherr. Soon, as the situation is clarified, the good doctor is happily prepping his new patients for surgery. He ushers the uninjured raiders out of the laboratory and tells Mr. Wilx to have them wait in the Dining Room upstairs while he tends to their friends.

Of course, the good doctor rationalizes the wounded men as an unexpected opportunity. He has just finished a set of iron casement steam pistoning arms and he can't let such an opportunity go to waste. He spends some precious time cleaning Luke's wounds and adding more metals than he removes as he repairs the damage done to the man's back by the shotgun pellets. The doctor grabs his bone saw and begins cutting out the weak flesh and replacing it with the superior iron and brass steam augmentations. He discards Luke's shattered arm with the same disdain that he shows Jim's undamaged arm. The raiders lie blissfully unconscious as Doctor Freiherr excises the weak flesh and implants hard, cold metal in its place.

That night, Colonel Jones, Mr. Wilx and Carl sit quietly at the dining room table drinking mugs of local beer and smoking cigars. Each man lost in his own thoughts; be they about the travesty of the train robbery or the wounded men downstairs in the doctor's laboratory. All three men silently thank providence for the fact that they can not see what the doctor will do in order to save the wounded men. All three are certain that the men will be saved from their injuries, but, none would volunteer to go under Doctor Freiherr's knife.

The Glass Coffin

Colonel Jones looks at Carl and tries to decide what to do with the raiders; his former soldiers. Despite his best efforts and intentions, he knows Doctor Freiherr does not have much chance of reversing his condition and he will forever eschew the sunlight. So be it. A lifetime beneath the moonlight is a small price to pay for the strengths gained and indeed his very existence after the unfortunate run in with Persephone. The old soldier in him knows that one day that score must be settled. For now, the colonel's vengeance can wait and having a ready made cavalry unit under roof could have its advantages in the new order of things.

'Carl, I think it would be best for you and your men to stay here at the estate for a while. While I am sure they will recover just fine, Luke and Jim will no doubt have need of Doctor Freiherr's ministrations beyond tonight's activities. I am sure I can find enough adventure and profit that you will not have to try such a dangerous expedition on your own again.'

'Thank you kindly, Colonel. Truth is we didn't fare that badly in spite of Jim and Luke's getting shot up a piece. I figure we left that train with at least $1,200.' So saying, the raider throws a heavy saddle bag onto the dining room table and gold coins and paper bills fall out of its opening.

Colonel Jones and Mr. Wilx stare at the money; both lost in their own thoughts. Carl, watching the looks on the men's faces smiles. He knows what the aristocratic colonel thinks of his hired help and can't help but enjoy the man's naked greed as he looks over Carl's saddlebag. Trust the rich, he thinks, to always want more riches.

'Carl, I must admit, I am impressed. I hadn't realized that your little adventure paid off so well. I do believe we can work on your tactics and lessen the risk a bit on your next raid. That is, if you don't mind taking advice from an old cavalry officer?' Colonel Jones finishes his question with a wide smile.

Carl and Mr. Wilx both grin at the veiled offer of assistance. Carl grins remembering the by gone war years and how the colonel's planning and leadership led them from victory to victory over the Southerners. Mr. Wilx grins, happy to see the vigor and life that has returned to the colonel since that horrible night when Mr. Wilx could not save him. The men drink and smoke far into the night discussing the perils and rewards of various scenarios for robbing trains. Carl thinks nothing is unusual when Colonel Jones becomes lethargic and has to excuse himself near daybreak. Mr. Wilx looks a little pale as the colonel slowly gets to his feet and shuffles out of the room; moving with all the slowness and carefulness of an Octogenarian.

The Mansion, August 1867

The colonel awakes the next night starving with a deep hunger he cannot identify. He passes by the Sitting Room and its waiting goblet. Tonight he thirsts for something more. He stalks out of the mansion and out to the courtyard like a man walking in his sleep. He sniffs the night air and listens to its sounds. Calmly, without quite knowing why, he walks steadily towards a small lantern light shining brightly, to his eyes inside the barn. His eyes glow in the darkness and he walks quietly and purposefully down the row of stalls until he comes up behind a livery boy busying himself with some menial task. The vampire colonel wraps the young servant in his strong arms and sinks his fangs deep in the youth's neck before he is aware of what he is doing. Instantly, Colonel Jones feels his chest warm, his limbs tingle and become stronger with every drop of blood. Electricity bursts throughout his nervous system and a rush of adrenaline overwhelms his senses. He feels his cold heart warm and his muscles contract and become denser, somehow stronger. The colonel holds the now dead servant boy out away from him and the euphoria fades with the cold knowledge that he has taken a life and worse that he has murdered one of his own servants. He

The Glass Coffin

stands in the darkness holding the boy not moving, not knowing what to do next.

Outside in the large courtyard two figures with lanterns exit the mansion and begin circling the grounds in different directions. The figures shine their lanterns around at the empty dirt road and the trees surrounding the mansion. Finally, Doctor Freiherr's raspy voice can be heard calling for the colonel. Mr. Wilx's deep bass voice echoes that call in the distance.

The colonel exits the barn wiping spittle and blood from the corners of his mouth. The gentleman soldier tries to wipe the dark blood stains from his shirt sleeves with his hands as he walks across the courtyard straight to the arch. He calls out to the doctor and stammers as he quietly tells the doctor of the stable boy's death and his undeniable desire to feed on living blood. A great frown and a sigh, he quietly tries to describe the feelings and electricity he felt when he fed on the stable boy's blood. The doctor nods reluctantly in mock understanding. Hesitantly, he takes hold of the colonel's arm and escorts him back into the mansion. He calmly informs the colonel that they must go down into the laboratory for some tests. In spite of the warm air, Colonel Jones shivers at the word 'tests', but, allows the doctor to guide him inside and down the long staircase.

A few minutes later, Doctor Freiherr walks back out of the mansion and finds Mr. Wilx still walking in the empty countryside. He calls out to Mr. Wilx and the two talk quietly as they stand by the short stone wall. Doctor Freiherr tells Mr. Wilx of the dead boy in the stable. The faithful manservant is given strange instructions by his master; he is told wrap the boy up in any old covering and wait outside thirty minutes before brining the body down to the laboratory. With this strange request, the doctor turns and walks back into the house leaving Mr. Wilx to stare after him for a moment before walking hesitantly into the dark interior of the barn.

Colonel Jones walks into the main floor's sitting room, just catching sight of Mr. Wilx as he enters the mansion carrying a burlap bundle over his shoulder. The big man grunts in greeting before walking past the colonel and down the staircase to the lower level and the laboratory.

Inside the sitting room, the raiders stand at Colonel Jones' entrance and raise their glasses in salute. Even Jim and Luke are smiling at their employer and benefactor. Conversation quickly breaks out into a jumble of voices as the men express their gratitude for the colonel's hospitality and on the effectiveness of Doctor Freiherr's improvements to Jim and Luke. The men are still marveling at the fact that both men are alive and at the power of their steam limbs when Doctor Freiherr enters the room. The men again rise and cheer the doctor for his marvelous medical prowess. Doctor Freiherr gives them a mock bow and is genuinely pleased at their appreciation and acceptance of his handiwork.

Colonel Jones sits quietly in an overstuffed chair watching the raiders praise the doctor. His own thoughts stay on the unfortunate stable boy and the incredible rejuvenating effects of the boy's blood. Slowly his squeamishness over the way he took the life from his faithful servant gives way to a darker hunger. The vampire starts to picture more raids under the night sky, not for gold or silver, but, for the richer treasure of blood.

Analytical Engine

The next night, the men are sitting and smoking cigars eager to relax after a fine meal when Mr. Wilx enters and tells the assembled men about a train shipment that he has heard about thru one of his many sources. The spy has heard talk of a wondrous mechanical engine designed to assist in complex computations and arithmetic endeavors. An Analytical Engine of some great size and bulk built up of cogs, gears and some unknown composition is being sent by train from New York to Boston. Doctor Freiherr's dark eyes light up at the thought of possessing and controlling such a machine. The doctor implores Colonel Jones to help him acquire the unique engine, as it would be just the right mechanism to greatly enhance his efforts at finding a cure to the colonel's condition. The doctor watches the man's mind weighing the expense and the risk of such a bold undertaking. The doctor smiles, knowing that in the end the colonel will eventually agree to anything to regain a seemingly normal lifestyle. While his host is thinking dollars versus the freedom of once more walking awake in the sunlight, the scientist is lost in mental imaginings and plans to use the machine for devising new experiments to create better men; iron men who will not tire and never need sleep.

The Glass Coffin

In the end, Colonel Jones agrees to consider any plans to acquire the computational engine. He listens intently and ponders what little information Mr. Wilx has gleaned from his unknown sources about the train's schedule and route. The raiders jump into the conversation; eager to add their recent expertise to the venture's planning.

Everyone soon agrees that this robbery will require more men be brought on for the actual raid. Oddly, it is Bob that suggests the hiring of an airship given the distance that they must travel and the size of the cargo they mean to seize. They all agree that a wagon will not be large enough or strong enough to carry their prize. The group spends some time trying to devise a scheme for stopping the train and how to recognize the engine when they board the baggage car where it will presumably be stored. Doctor Freiherr leaves the room, taking the two raiders with the steam arms with him assuring everyone that they will be more than ready and even more capable when next they are needed. The raider leader, Carl looks concerned over this last announcement. But, he is intelligent enough to know he has no real power in this gathering.

Col Jones, Carl and Mr. Wilx sit down to discuss the logistics needed for such an unfamiliar and risky undertaking, Colonel Jones announces that the men will not be able to ride their horses that far and then back again to the mansion in a single day. No they must devise a new plan for after they have raided the train to make their getaway and quite probably will need a new method for stopping the train. The raider leader looks at the gleam in Colonel Jones' eyes as the military officer begins to warm to the idea and fall back into bygone days of military planning and tactics. He knows full well what can happen in the field when the plans are poorly planned or tried for the first time. Someone else will be hurt or worse; fall beneath the doctor's knives.

As the plan begins to take place, all three men realize the complexity and the expense that will be required. Colonel Jones begins to smile and the other men look at him in open wonder. The veteran cavalryman sits back in his chair and lights a cigar making a single statement, 'It would seem gentlemen we will need to secure a source of outside financing for this undertaking. Yes, a source of quick cash that can be used to purchase the men and supplies needed to acquire the Doctor's Analytical Engine. Oh, and of course, should there be any left over well profit is always encouraged in business ventures.'

'Colonel, what exactly do you mean?' Carl asks with trepidation in his voice.

'Simply put, I believe it is time for your men to take another train for a ride. Only, I do believe, I will accompany you on this venture. I do feel a strong urge to get out of this mausoleum and back into the game as it were. Mr. Wilx, do any of your marvelous sources know where we could find a suitable train carrying possibly a payroll for a coal mine and most importantly, traveling at night?' says the Colonel while working his way into an evil grin.

'I am sure, if such a train exists, I can find out when and where, sir' says Mr. Wilx.

'Then, gentlemen, with your pardon, I do believe I will take a walk in the courtyard before retiring for the night,' says the colonel.

The Night Train

In the Massachusetts countryside far between two stations, a bonfire burns brightly on the railroad tracks. Out in the dark amongst the ever green trees, Colonel Jones and the raiders sit atop their horses waiting.

Colonel Jones rides ahead of the other raiders away from the tree line and into the tall grass. He sits atop a midnight black stallion and smiles at the empty rails, as clear to him as if the noon sun were out and not a quarter moon. He spots the tiny headlamp of the train and soon can see the rivets on the engine and the stovepipe smokestack as the train hurtles down the tracks at forty miles an hour. While still too dim for the raiders to see it, the colonel has no problem seeing the coal car, the baggage car behind it and now that they have come around the bend a line of passenger cars comes into his view as well. He watches silently as the headlamp grows larger and brighter. He unholsters his pistol and waves to the men in the trees; forgetting for a moment that they are possessed of a much more limited view. He is about to call out to them when the train's engineer catches his first glimpse of the bonfire's light and blasts the steam whistle in warning. The colonel turns to ride back to the raiders and misses the first wave of sparks as the engineer applies the brakes.

The raiders can now hear the whistle and make out the lone headlamp, but, they miss the shower of sparks leaping from the train's iron wheels as the brakes clamp down hard. The train is still moving a fair clip as it approaches the bonfire. No doubt its conductors are busy running down the cars applying more brakes and trying to calm the passengers. This time all the raiders can hear the squeal of brakes and the harsh steam whistle as the engineer recognizes the light from the bonfire for what it is and reacts to the danger to the train. Inside the passenger cars, men and women are jolted off their feet or thrown against the benches as the brakes bring the train to a stop.

The train screeches to a halt at almost the same moment in time as the Colonel raises his pistol and orders the raiders to ride towards the train. The colonel watches Luke ride past him and straight for the train's engine. The bearded Luke rides hard and fast; a curious itching in his back reminding him of the last time he rode at a train and the fierce pain he suffered from that encounter. This engineer and stoker don't have time to react as Luke leaps off his horse and climbs into the engine compartment with a murderous intent. The young stoker tries to swing his shovel, but, it is batted away by Luke's iron arm. He draws his percussion pistol and shoots the stoker in the chest and then the elderly engineer without hesitation. He leans back out of the cab and waves as the other four raiders ride past to the baggage car.

Jim, who has also received Doctor Freiherr's obscene ministrations uses his bulky steam driven arm to twist open the locked door of the baggage car. The lanky man has a moment of trouble disconnecting his clawed hand from the door's handle. While he is indisposed, Colonel Jones enthusiastically jumps into the car. He rolls across the wooden planks of the floor with his percussion cap and ball pistols spitting flame and lead in the dim light of the car's interior. A couple of minutes later and Carl has joined the colonel. He sees the baggage handler lying dead in a pool of blood and the Colonel trying to open the safe. Unfortunately for him, the baggage handler's keys do not seem to fit the black and red iron safe. Carl hesitates for seconds only before yelling for Jim to come into the baggage car. The iron armed raider is again put to good use as he rips the safe door from its hinges. At the sight of bags of coins and an impressive stack of treasury notes, the raiders cheer; even the normally stoic Colonel Jones is caught up in the moment and laughs aloud as he quietly drops the baggage handler's ring of keys. The raiders quickly begin grabbing money and the paper bills and bags of coins. Leaving only Carl inside to further search, the raiders exit the baggage car.

Meanwhile two passengers, six shooters drawn walk from the lead passenger car towards the engine intent on finding out why the train is stopped. They dimly catch sight of the raiders as they exit the lantern lit interior of the baggage car and shout to them. Colonel Jones' superior night vision allows him to see the two men clearly. He turns and fires his pistol twice, doubling up one man as the minie ball grazes his side drawing blood. The other passenger fires repeatedly in return; one lucky shot finds the Colonel in the dark.

Blinding pain and fire erupts in the colonel's chest and he falls to the ground. He cries out once in pain and then in anger. The vampire soldier feels a rage he has never known swell up inside him as he jumps to his feet. The pistol in his curled hand forgotten, the vampire colonel rushes up to the men in a blur of motion.

The wounded man tries to aim his pistol while his left hand holds his side. The colonel sniffs the air smelling the fresh blood and reaches out knocking the man to the ground with the butt of his pistol. The vampire turns and pistol whips the other man; knocking him heavily to the ground. The colonel looks at the men before holstering his pistol. The smell of blood fills his nostrils as the colonel grabs a handful of the wounded man's jacket and picks him up effortlessly. The man comes back to consciousness only to scream at the hellish face before him. The vampire colonel growls just before he sinks his newly grown fangs hungrily into the man's neck. Warm, rich blood floods the vampire colonel's body; he feels the man's pulse slowing down while his own cold heart seems to beat again as warmth spreads throughout his limbs. The pain in his chest dissipates and he reaches a clawed hand into the wound and removes the misshapen lead remains of a .36 caliber minie ball. Feeling light headed with formless energies rolling thru his veins; the colonel shoves the blood soaked lead ball into his victim's gasping mouth. He lets the dying man fall back onto the tall grass and laughs. His every sense alive and tingling, Colonel Jones lifts his arms to the heavens savoring the strange feelings even as they threaten to overwhelm him. With his eyes closed, the ex-cavalry officer can hear the other raiders murmuring behind him in surprise and fear. He smiles at their fear, at the thundering of their heartbeats in the darkness. He hears the soles of their boots slap the metal of their stirrups as they mount their horses, eager to leave. The vampire colonel sighs and calms himself before opening blood tinged eyes. He glides unnaturally over to his horse before swinging effortlessly into the saddle. Once more the gentleman colonel, Jones spurs his horse and rides swiftly for the tree line. The other men gallop in line behind him. They are still shaken, but, have little choice now but to follow him back to the mansion.

It is sometime later when the first passengers led by a conductor venture forth from the train's well lit interior and walk the tracks up to the engine. They have almost recovered from the grizzly sight of the dead engineer and young stoker when a man comes out of the darkness shouting about vampires and raiders that will not die when shot. The passengers try to calm the man and then follow him to a patch of flattened grass shaped like a sleeping man; empty save for a bowler hat and a spotlessly clean mangled lead minie ball. The conductor picks up the pistol's bullet and frowns at the small teeth marks; he holds it out to the other passengers just as the strange man who led them to it faints.

A Midnight Ride in the Country

Colonel Jones enters the mansion's Dining Room just after dark to find Mr. Wilx talking to Carl while the other men drink beer and finish the last of what looks to be a fine meal. Carl stands immediately as the colonel enters and the other men sit up straight in their chairs; only Mr. Wilx smiles.

'Gentlemen, please at ease. Kindly return to your meals. I did not mean to disturb you, but, I feel I must make amends for my behavior last night at the train. I realize being shot in the chest is a strange excuse for the shall we say excessive actions I took. I cannot tell you what came over me, but, I want to assure each and every one of you that you are safe in my company and as valued guests under my roof,' says the colonel a bit sheepishly.

'Colonel Jones, Mr. Wilx has been explaining to us the unique disease that you are plagued with. I and all the men offer our sincerest best wishes for a speedy recovery. While I will not pretend to understand what you are going thru or what exactly transpired at the train, I do believe you when you say we are safe; as I believed Mr. Wilx when he also stated that fact earlier today,' says Carl.

'I thank you, Carl. And what of the rest of you; Jim, Luke, Edwin are you convinced of my sincerity and your safety? I would not want to replace any of you, but, I will not have you stay here out of fear.'

'Colonel, Jim and I owe you and Doctor Freiherr our lives; we cannot leave,' says Luke.

'I work for Carl, sir, and he works for you. Since the war ended, Carl's kinda been taking care of us; so if he says stay then I stay,' says Edwin his face breaking into a nervous grin.

'Good news, that. Well, I hate to dash off, but, with Mr. Wilx's help I have some errands to run this night. I do thank you all for your loyalty.' So saying, the gray haired ex-soldier turns sharply on his heels and walks back out of the room and out the front door to the courtyard. Mr. Wilx excuses himself and walks outside himself.

'That went better than I thought it would. I am sure I owe that to you, Mr. Wilx.'

'You are most welcome, colonel.'

Mr. Wilx stands stock still holding the horses hitched to the wagon in the courtyard as a very spry Colonel Jones springs up onto the wagon and picks up the reins.

'Thank you for hitching up the horses, Mr. Wilx. I believe I shall take a ride into town tonight. Please give my regrets to Carl and the others.'

'Yes, Colonel. I will be sure to inform them that you have been called away on business. I mean no disrespect, but, Doctor Freiherr made me promise to remind you of the talk you had.'

'Do not fear, faithful Mr. Wilx. I will heed the doctor's warning and be back long before sunrise. And tell him I have not forgotten my promise. Should I find any game worth hunting tonight, I will be sure to bring the carcass back for his inspection. Now, please do not think me rude, but, I am in a hurry to be off.'

'Surely, sir. Oh, and I would give the woods a wide berth if'n I was you. The center of the road would be the safe course from now on. Doctor Freiherr has a few experiments running in the woods that it would be best to avoid.'

'Oh, I had not heard that. Thank you, Mr. Wilx.'

So saying, the colonel smiles revealing pointed teeth in a toothy smile as the horses take off across the courtyard and out to the dirt road. He hears a low moaning noise coming from somewhere in the trees to his right side, but, heeding the warning from Mr. Wilx, pays it no attention and continues towards the small town nearby.

It is almost an hour later when the colonel dismounts and securely applies the brake to the wagon's wheel. He leaves the wagon and its team of horses alongside the trees and stalks confidently down the dirt lane beneath the moonlight. Should he be seen, he thinks, he can easily explain a visit to town after being absent these past weeks.

It is only when he is inside the sleeping town and spots a couple kissing behind one of the one story wood houses that his excitement is aroused. He quickly vanishes behind a large oak tree and looks closer at the young couple. A quick intact of breath as he recognizes the girl as young Constance the maid. He has thought to wonder what became of her after that dreadful night; well, he thinks, this shall be fun. The vampire soldier glides across the grass somehow moving from shadow to shadow growing ever closer to the couple. He hears the cheerful giggling and then smiles as Constance closes her eyes so her young beau can kiss her. He moves to the left and comes up behind the young man and raises his arms.

With a mighty force, the vampire grabs the boy by his shoulders and throws him to the ground; knocking the youngster unconscious with a swift booted kick to the head. Constance's eyes open in confusion and then wider in fear as she sees the man's hungry face and shining pearl white fangs. The one time servant and maid opens her mouth to scream, but, Colonel Jones reaches forward and clamps a hand over her mouth with a vice like grip and roughly twists her head to one side before sinking his fangs deep into her neck. He sighs with the first taste of the rushing blood; made all the more potent by the adrenaline pumping thru her frightened body. It is the old man's turn to close his eyes demurely as he feeds on the young woman's life blood. Fireworks flare behind his eyes and the girl's blood courses thru him awakening all his muscles and nerves at once. All too soon, the girl is drained, both her life and her supply of blood vanishing beneath the vampire's gluttony. The colonel is about to drop the corpse when Mr. Wilx's words and his promise to Doctor Freiherr come back to him. Instead, the colonel throws the maid's corpse over his shoulder and effortlessly bends over and grabs the unconscious boy by his collar. Still only slightly burdened, the colonel begins his slow walk back to the wagon and a comfortable ride back to the mansion with his gifts for Doctor Freiherr. All in the name of science, he thinks to himself chuckling.

'

Bureau of Military Information, New York City, August

1867

Two men in their twenties stand together in quiet

conversation outside of a heavy wooden office door. The

blond haired Lieutenant Sterling tries to adjust his

oversized wool suit jacket seeking to hide the metal of his

prosthetic, steam driven left arm. A victim of a bullet in

the arm during the recent War Between the States, the

twenty four year old young man is self conscious of his

iron and steam replacement limb. Sterling's crude clawed

metal fingers curl and uncurl on the own clanking in time

to the sound of small hisses of steam. Still, he cannot stop

staring at a young raven haired woman as she types on a

mechanical machine at her desk. His friend, Lieutenant

Archibald Rawlings sees Sterling's discomfort and soon

finds its cause in the sly glances from the young lady in

question back at the two men, as well as the unladylike way

that she has crossed her legs and allowed her long dress to

creep up past her shapely ankles. The ever incorrigible

Rawlings smiles an evil smile and ponders how he can add

to Reginald's discomfort without breaking the silent spell.

A balding, heavy set gentleman in a black wool suit

suddenly opens the office door and motions for the two

young men to come inside. The older man adjusts his shirt

collar and then the stifling tie and sits heavily in a claw footed leather chair behind a mahogany desk and looks towards the young men standing in front of him. Sterling and Rawlings keep their heads still as they glance around them at the oak walled office. Both men take in the large picture of President Jackson on the wall behind the older man. Their eyes move and take in the gilded framed paintings of county landscapes and quaint cottages. They notice the room's single window on the far side of the large room; its light cleaner somehow than the yellow gaslight that bathes their side of the room. The heavy set man leans forward to address his guests.

'Lieutenant Sterling, Lieutenant Rawlings, a good morning to you both.'

'Good morning, Superintendent James, sir.'

'Yes, well, let's get right to business. Gentlemen, please do sit down. I've asked you to attend me on a most important matter. There is to be a delivery made from New York to the Bureau's Boston District. We have been fortunate enough to obtain a second Analytical Engine of Babbage's design and are giving it to the Boston District; where they will put it to good use. There is a top rate group of professors in Boston that have shown great aptitude with smaller mechanical computing devices. Officially, we are hoping to increase our computers' abilities by setting up the second Engine and doubling our computers' access to an Analytical Engine. The Bureau has also graciously offered to assemble and install the Analytical Engine without a representative of Her Majesty's Government having to make the arduous crossing from England. Unofficially, we are quite certain that the Boston Bureau can map out the Engine's design and components well enough engineer a similar design and use the factories and tradesmen in Boston to build an Analytical Engine of American manufacture and thus end our dependence on England for the manufacture and shipment of the frightfully expensive engines' says the Superintendent with a wolfish grin.

'Most intriguing, sir, but, I don't know a two cent piece worth about the workings of an Analytical Engine and I didn't know Mr. Sterling had any aptitude in that area either' says the taller of the two young men with a smile.

'Ha. Nicely put, Rawlings. No, you two gentleman will be accompanying, chaperoning actually, the crates on their journey by rail from New York to Boston's South Station. Once the cargo is safely unloaded at Boston, a local detachment will take possession and you gentlemen will be free of responsibility' says Superintendent James.

'Ah, I see. Superintendent, no offence, I would think you would want a tad bit more muscle in the chaperone department for such a valuable cargo. Not that Archie and I couldn't handle any unpleasantness that arose, but, sending us alone does show rather more confidence in our abilities that is perhaps warranted' says Lieutenant Rawlings.

'Hmph. You must think me senile, Mister Rawlings. There will be a heavily armed squad of Union Army soldiers riding with the crates in the box car. That is the muscle portion of the protection detail that I would like to go quietly unnoticed. You two fine fellows are the Bureau's official chaperones should anyone learn of the shipment. You two will ride with the other passengers on the train and be a focus for the attentions of anyone curious about the cargo. I need two intelligent, sophisticated operatives to ride with the other passengers and watch for signs of suspicious behavior amongst the other passengers; while the clockwork Analytical Engine rides safely in the company of the soldiers who will also ride in one of the train's boxcars with the crates. Unfortunately, I don't have two sophisticated, talented fellows at the moment and instead have decided to hand the job over to the two of you.'

A quick, rapid knocking at the door interrupts the young men's simultaneous outbursts of indignation. While not certain exactly how, the two men are quite certain that somewhere in that mission statement was an insult to their character and abilities.

'Superintendent, coffee is served at your pleasure.'

'Yes, please bring it in, Miss Wilkshire.'

The same lovely, black haired woman that so distressed Sterling earlier enters the room dressed in a conservative bustled dress and white cotton blouse buttoned to the neck carrying a silver serving set with three bone china coffee cups. She glides into the room and all three men stand up, Rawlings and Sterling having to turn around to avoid being rude. Miss Wilkshire looks directly at young Sterling and smiles warmly before turning and crossing the room to a low oak coffee table surrounded by high backed chairs. He is still staring at her as she bends over and places the silver set on the low coffee table. She looks back over her shoulder and he begins to blush at the smile on her face. Miss Wilkshire stands and with her face calm and business like, the young lady turns around nodding to the superintendent before exiting the room without a word. The three men move to take a seat around the coffee table; lured by the heady aroma of fresh brewed coffee. There is only the sound of clinking china and the pouring of coffee and fresh milk for a moment while all three get their coffee prepared. Then the men begin discussing the details of the shipment to Boston and the exact nature of the Lieutenants Rawlings and Sterling's responsibilities and options should anything happen during the train's long journey. Both men set their coffee down for a moment when the Superintendent tells them about a recent train robbery in the Massachusetts countryside and the rather unique description of a vampire train robber and metal armed raiders. Lieutenants Sterling and Rawlings both look at the older man in disbelief, but, can not bring themselves to be so rude as to question the Superintendent's sanity in his own office.

New York City Train Station, August 1867

Lieutenants Sterling and Rawlings stand pleasantly chatting at the New York Train Station; carefully not watching the large crates as they are being loaded into a box car. Nor do they hazard a look at the soldiers that follow the crate into the box car and do not exit as it is closed and locked. Sterling once again denies his attraction to Miss Wilkshire and once again his friend voices disbelief. Sterling is about to protest too much when Rawlings elbows him in the right side and nods towards a comely young blond lady and her stern looking chaperone as they climb aboard the train.

'Stay focused for once, please Archie.' Sterling says.

'I am focused Reginald old friend. Focused on separating that fair maiden from her respectability and you could well help me in that endeavor should you focus on separating her from her evil chaperone.'

Sterling laughs, 'A priceless Difference Engine, a squad of soldiers hidden in a boxcar on the train; not to mention our worthy selves sent from the New York Society's Operations Center on our first mission to guard said boxcar. All the while being on the alert for, if that one report is to be believed; a uniformed vampire leading a band of ex-copperhead southern sympathizing train robbers in the countryside of Massachusetts and all you can focus on is a maiden in need of losing her virtue to your carnal lusts. I ask you, however did I get partnered with such a cad as you, Mr. Archibald Rawlings?'

'The reason for such a pairing should be obvious, Reginald my poor serious compatriot. I have been sent by providence itself to redeem a dull and unimaginative half man-half steam engine man such as yourself and show you the opportunities that life presents.'

'Now, come along and let's grab a seat where I can keep an eye on the future Mrs. Archibald Rawlings.'

'Oh, so it is matrimony you are after. My apologies, I did mistake your intentions, you are a gentleman after all.'

'Nonsense, my good fellow. I'm sure that should you one day meet a lady who will look past that steam furnace you wear on your shoulder, you will need your old friend Reggie to instruct you in the finer points of romance.'

'Steam furnace…This furnace is going to flatten that too smug face of yours one day.'

The pair break into laughter as Sterling lifts his bulky, iron left arm clumsily and makes to swing at his friend. Both men spare one moment to look about the station and at the box car before they board the train and leave New York behind. In the shadows near the train station's entrance, the raven haired Miss Wilkshire watches the young men board the train. The young Bureau operative silently wishes the men well before opening her parasol in an attempt to block some of the falling ash from the train's smoke stack and heavy water vapors from its steam engine as the train begins slowly chugging its way away from the station.

The Glass Coffin

Outside Salem, August 1867

The train's swaying motion has at some point put Sterling
fast asleep. He only realizes this as he awakens. He tries
to sit up straighter in his seat and looks around him quickly.
He looks out the nearby window and sees huge fields of
green grass and a distant line of elm and oak trees going
past. From the sun's position in the fair blue sky, the
young man guesses the train should be somewhere in the
Massachusetts countryside near its destination by now. He
looks down the red carpeted aisle at his fellow passengers;
then tries to get comfortable. The high back bench with its
leather seat covering and minimal padding does little for
his comfort; though it was obviously not uncomfortable
enough to keep him awake.

Sterling smiles at the elder gentleman sitting across
from him. From his top hat, wide white cravat with its
diamond pin to his gray vest, waist coat and loose gray
creased trousers, Sterling guesses the man to be a banker
returning to Boston from some business or another in New
York.

The fetching young lady sitting with the older man
is more of a mystery. Her black hair is properly pinned up
and its thick tresses partially hidden beneath a wide
brimmed expensive hat. Her ample bosom with its sun

browned skin is clearly visible above the dress line of her navy blue dress which billows out to either side of what he is sure are well defined dancer's legs. She studiously avoids making direct eye contact with any gentleman on the train, save only her escort. Yet, the red rouge on her cheeks, also browned by the sun, the dark red lipstick seem to be applied a trifle too thick to be properly ladylike. And the ladies dark eyes have a mischievous twinkle that strikes young Sterling as most unladylike.

This last thought leads Sterling's mind to Rawlings and the question of his whereabouts. He spies his erstwhile partner sitting at a table at the far end of the passenger car with the young lady from the train station and her chaperone. It appears to Sterling's shocked eyes that Rawlings has somehow charmed both women. He can not hear the conversation, but, can not mistake both women's look of rapt attention or the way the younger woman is laughing at something Rawlings just said. Sterling's wakening hunger and an uncharacteristic touch of mischief causes the young man to stand, excuse himself from the banker and his mistress and walk down the aisle way to Rawlings as he sits engrossed in conversation at the table.

'Reggie, fancy meeting you here! I was just on my way to the Dining Car. Do come with me chum, we simply must take lunch and become reacquainted.'

'Uh, quite. Miss Inthrope, Miss Construe, allow me to introduce my associate Mr. Reginald Sterling. Unfortunately, Mr. Sterling was injured during the war and hasn't been right in the head since then. I assure you the monstrous brass and iron arm is the least of the poor man's deformities.'

'Now, Archie, I must protest. I merely stopped to offer my country cousin a free meal. I have no doubt, your finances being what they are…You have taken care of that awful gambling fiasco by now, no doubt…that you probably spent your last dollar booking passage on this fine train.'

'Uh, really Penelope, Miss Construe. That is quite untrue. I have no gambling problem; I don't even wager. I am quite solidly employed, as Mr. Sterling knows full well.'

The sullen, disapproving looks from both women cause Rawlings' voice to dry up and he stands at the table looking imploringly at his friend. Sterling looks at the two ladies and swears the temperature at the table has dropped several degrees. He fully expects frost to come out with his breath as he bids the ladies farewell and walks quickly out of the car and into the adjoining Dining Car. Hurriedly he finds an empty table and seats himself with a heavy thud. Anxious and a nervous, he bursts into laughter.

Sterling has calmed down somewhat and is busily admiring the dark oak walls and large glass windows when Rawlings stomps up to the table and throws himself into the chair opposite him. The sad look on his friend's face forces a giggle out of Sterling and a definite pain begins to form in his side from holding in the laughter.

'That was most unfair of you, old man. I had to do some fast talking to salvage the ladies' good opinion of me. An opinion I worked very hard to create before you walked up and ruined it. Oh, by the way, should either of them ask later, you have just been released from Our Mother of the Sacred Heart Asylum in upstate New York.'

'OH, my. Horribly disfigured and insane. Why ever do you put up with me, old friend?'

'Excuse me, gentlemen. Have you decided what you will be having today?'

The two young men look the porter up and down at his immaculate white uniform and white gloves; looking for all the world to them like an attendant in an insane asylum. They exchange a look with each other and burst into laughter; the laughs becoming more uncontrollable at the poor man's confused expression.

Their dinner repast finished, Sterling and Rawlings make their way back to Miss Inthrope and Miss Construe's table. The men apologize and try to convince the women that their antics meant no insult to either lady. The two women are quite forgiving once a somber Sterling explains the truth of their deception. Sterling tries to conceal his metal claw hand while he sits talking pleasantly with Miss Construe. Both of them shake their heads slightly as Rawlings is once again entertaining Miss Inthrope with fictitious tales of his gallantry in the recent war. Lieutenant Rawlings is getting to the point in the story where he saves General Grant's life when all four of them are thrown forward by the train's sudden deceleration. The squeal of the brakes ends any conversation and the men and women are thrown together as the train comes to an abrupt stop. Sterling awkwardly releases his grip on Miss Inthrope's waist and turns his face burning with an inner heat. Rawlings is less abrupt in settling Miss Construe back into her seat. He looks at the blushing red glow of Miss Inthrope's face and sees its twin on Sterling. Rawlings smiles before looking around at the rest of the passenger car. The air is alive with shouts of concern and confusion as the rest of the passengers pick themselves up off the carpeted floor or try to disengage themselves from their neighbors. Several men press their face to the frosted glass windows trying to get a look outside at the cause for the sudden stop. One look at empty countryside and everyone is convinced this was not a scheduled stop for the train. Rawlings nods his head at Sterling while drawing his revolver. Sterling answers his nod with one of his own and drawing his LeMat pistol heads for the rear of the passenger car. Just the sight of the metal armed man and the drawn pistol is enough to form a wave of emptiness in front of him as he walks to the rear of the car. Rawlings wastes no time running the short distance to the end of the car and bolting outside.

Sterling hops out the back doorway of the car and races towards the boxcar while Rawlings takes up position outside the passenger car facing the engine. He can't see the cause for their sudden stop from where he is and so starts walking towards the front of the train.

Sterling uses the butt of his pistol to rap on the boxcar door until it is opened from within. An anxious looking private throws open the door and two other soldiers thrust their rifles out at the surprised Sterling.

'Hold on there men, at ease. I am Lieutenant Sterling, Bureau of Military Information. I am your contact on the train.'

'Begging your pardon, sir. What's going on, why has the train stopped?'

'I don't know private, but, I aim to find out. For right now, I want everyone to file out and take up guard around the boxcar till we get the situation sorted out. Corporal form a skirmish line and keep an eye towards those trees.'

So saying, Sterling turns around and begins running for the front of the train. He is past their passenger car and halfway along the next car when he catches up with Rawlings returning from the front of the train. Rawling stops when he sees Sterling and stands stock still quietly waiting for his friend to reach him. The stalled train does not worry Sterling as much as the serious expression on his friend's face and the silence.

'Reggie, what's the matter man?'

'Look for yourself. The track ahead has been blown up. I might not be a real war hero such as yourself, but, I know a hole left by explosives when I see one.'

'What... who would do that?'

The answer comes in the form of a dozen fast riding horsemen already halfway across the field from the tall old ever green trees and riding hard for the train. The horsemen must see the two operatives because they start shooting. Rawlings and Sterling run for the side of the train and crouch down seeking to make smaller targets out of themselves. Knowing the distance is too far for an accurate shot, the men hold their fire trusting in the horsemen to narrow the distance for them.

Seeing one of the horsemen ride up next to the engine compartment and draw his pistol, Rawlings raises his revolver; cocks back the hammer and fires. He doesn't wait to see where the bullet went, but, cocks the hammer and fires; twice more. Beside him, Sterling aims at the bunch of horsemen still riding fast towards the baggage car and fires his LeMat pistol several times into the crowd trusting more in luck than aim.

Bullets kick up dirt at Rawlings feet and both men are hit by wood splinters as bullets from the horsemen's pistols hit the passenger car behind them. The two young men drop to the ground and fire their pistols while lying flat in the tall grass.

The horsemen dismount and rush into the baggage car. Rawlings and Sterling hear shots fired inside the baggage car. The raiders exit the car agitated and confused. The raiders look past Sterling at the soldiers in front of the boxcar and the truth comes to them in a flash.

From the nearby woods, three figures in gray capes walk ponderously towards the soldiers and the boxcar making no effort at guile. The three waddle stiffly towards the soldiers, small smoke clouds puffing up from behind them. Soon, the soldiers can clearly see the miniature furnaces powering steam engines mounted on their iron men's backs. Sterling stares at the brass gears spinning while the iron men chug and clank their way thru the tall grass. Sterling frowns in vague recognition and his face twitches as he sees the iron men raise their ponderous brass and iron arms and open and close their metal claws. The dozen or so raiders outside the baggage car begin firing using the diversion of the iron men to their advantage.

Instantly following the barked commands from their corporal, the soldiers drop to one knee and lay down a storm of lead bullets in a display of disciplined black powder rifle fire. Two of the raiders spin around with the impact of bullets and fall to the ground dead. The rest fall prone to the ground or run back to the relative safety of the baggage car.

Sterling and Rawlings turn to face the slow moving iron men and begin taking pistol shots at them. Sparks fly as some of their bullets hit the mark only to ricochet off metal joints or limbs.

Leaving the flesh and bone raiders to the soldiers, Rawlings and Sterling run across the field to meet the new threat from the most unnatural foes. Even close up, it is hard for either man to find enough flesh to make their pistol shots effective. Somehow, the men have been clad in a living suit of armor; though surely not all of their flesh has been replaced by iron. Sterling ducks under a ponderous iron arm as it swings at him and thrusts his own arm up into the iron man's face. The iron mask dents and he is rewarded with a cry of pain from the man beneath it. Sterling grins; then rolls across the ground as the iron man pulls both his arms downward trying to drive Sterling's shoulders into the ground.

Rawlings pistol is empty and hitting the iron man with it just seems to aggravate the man beneath the iron mask. He falls back out of reach of the steam piston arms and desperately tries to think of a new tactic. He is still dodging the iron man's clumsy punches when the third iron man; forgotten about until now, hits Rawlings knocking him sideways and to the ground. Rawlings pulls a small pepperbox pistol from his waistcoat and lurches back to his feet. His ribs scream in protest at each breath. The man tries not to take a deep breath as he ducks under the first iron man's swinging arms and coming up right next to its chest; thrusts the pepperbox's barrels up against the iron man's eye slit and fires. The iron man's head snaps back and he falls noisily and loudly to the ground dead.

Sterling bats an iron arm aside with his own steam augmented arm and thrusts his pistol sword like at the iron man's neck. He triggers the single shotgun shell in the LeMat pistol and it explodes thru the iron man's leather encased neck; killing him. He screams and turns towards the remaining iron man; just at it takes another swipe at the prone figure of Rawlings.

Sterling raises his left arm high and shouts out to the iron man. The barrel shaped nightmare of metal and flesh turns away from Rawlings and takes two steps towards Sterling. They meet in a flash of metal and a loud crash as Sterling's metal arm meets the iron man's. Sterling twirls to the right and sees his steam piston arm bend most unnaturally as it stops a blow from the iron man meant to decapitate him. He dances back away from the iron man's clumsy swings; faster than his armored foe. Again he uses his left arm to bat aside a clumsy swing.

Sterling's his eyes go wide with fear and shock as his already damaged arm bends away once more breaking open the casing. He holds his left arm out in front of him and hot, live steam shoots out into the face of the iron man. He holds the arm steadily in the iron man's face even as he twists and turns to avoid its blindly swinging arms and clanking claws. Soon, the steam gone, his left arm falls heavily to his side. But, it has done its job; the last iron man is stomping from one foot to the other in pain; blinded by the live steam and unable to see his foe.

The blind juggernaut screams in rage and pain, its arms thrashing around in the air, blindly seeking Sterling. But, his left arm ruined and his pistol empty, the Bureau operative has moved safely out of reach and is standing beside his friend looking around at the impromptu battlefield. Rawlings sits in the tall grass, holding his wounded side with his right arm and breathing shallowly. At the boxcar three soldiers still remain standing. There is no sign of the raiders other than the dead and dying lying in the tall grass. The empty countryside's normal silence is marred by the moans and cries of the wounded.

Sterling walks back to the train, supporting Rawlings as best he can. His friend's face has an unhealthy pallor and he still can't seem to catch his breath. The soldiers ask what assistance can they render and Sterling points to the still marauding blind juggernaut in the distance. 'Kill It!' he says with a poison in his voice no one can mistake.

Inside the passenger car, Rawlings is laid on a bench seat near Miss Construe's table. Sterling sends the porter in search of a sawbones, if one is on the train. Outside, the soldiers surround the iron man and Sterling smiles when he hears the sound of rapid gunfire. He pats Rawlings on the shoulder and turns to exit the car again. He looks back at his friend and is pleased to see the young blond and her aunt rushing to help Rawlings and make him comfortable.

Standing alone outside, Sterling is trying to bind the dead metal of his twisted arm to his side when he hears a new sound. He cocks his head to one side and listens more intently to the muted clicking of a telegraph key. Sterling walks in a circle slowly zeroing in on the sound. A shout from one of the surviving soldiers is met by an angry look and frantic hand gestures to keep quiet. Finally, nearing a riderless horse with an oversized saddle bag, Sterling finds the source of the clicking noise.

Sterling opens the saddle bag, noticing the long trailing copper wire that is dragging the ground beside the horse. He hesitantly removes a large brass box what looks to him like five piano keys attached in front and sets it gently on the ground. He reaches back into the saddle bag and removes a second brass box with a wheel of paper tape attached to its side and a small rectangle screen built above it. He sets the larger box beside the first and frowns in concentration. Gently, he takes hold of a length of punched paper tape already trailing out of the box. He breaks off the paper tape and feeds it into a slot on the other side of the brass box. The box whirs with the sound of tiny gears and the rectangle comes to life with white letters against a black background. The message that appears on the visual display unit chills his bones. 'Carl, answer me. This is Doctor Freiherr. What is your status? What of the Analytical Engine? Is it safe?'

Sterling almost falls, his knees suddenly weak. He pushes himself up and then steps away from the wireless teletype engine, bewildered. He scans the trees in the now dark countryside and looks for any sign of life. In the distance rising above the trees, the stunned young man sees an airship rising and turning slowly around. He wonders if the hated Doctor Freiherr is aboard. Sterling is still staring at slow moving airship when he shouts for a soldier to come to him. The veteran soldier keeps his eyes steady on the departing airship as he points back to the brass boxes and orders the soldier to put them back into the saddle bag. He turns slowly and motions for the soldier to follow him. Together, they walk to the boxcar and carefully put the saddle bag onto the floor of the boxcar. The soldier is shocked at the hatred on Sterling's face as the Lieutenant tells him to guard the strange contraption. The soldier watches as the Lieutenant rubs his dead metal arm and walks back into the nearest passenger car of the train.

Sterling talks briefly to a railroad conductor and sends him and another of the surviving soldiers off on two of the raiders' horses into the night. Sterling has no doubt that the men will make it to the Salem train station and bring back help. He walks back inside the train and looks on as a prominent Boston surgeon professionally examines Rawlings bruised ribs. A ghost of a smile crosses his solemn face at the lively exclamations that the surgeon's touch elicits from his friend. Miss Construe and her aunt look properly serious and concerned as they help the sawbones by turning Rawlings and holding him steady while the physician tapes his ribs in place. Sterling walks to the boxcar and under the questioning eyes of the two remaining soldiers sits in the boxcar's doorway and quietly tries to reload his pistol one handed. He is still trying to make the shells fit into the pistol's chambers when he passes out.

Under the Knife Again

Sterling awakes on an operating table beneath a bright mirrored light of some kind. He tries to remember how he got here. Images swim rapidly across his mind. He sees a train from Salem arriving with a platoon of soldiers and plain clothes inspectors and policemen moving the passengers to the other train while a small crew carefully moves the boxcar's crates to the other train and another boxcar. Sterling vaguely remembers being helped onto the other train and lying down on a padded bench seat and drifting off to sleep. He tries to turn his head, but, it is held immobile. He tries to sit up and can't. He sees his arms rise up and panics at the shiny arm on his left side. It is too sleek and new to be his and he wonders what has happened while he slept. He begins to panic and then remembers more; a fight against iron men and his arm all but torn off of him. The panic begins to well up inside him and he cries out for help.

Sterling rolls his eyes left and right until a stocky brunette woman in a crisp white nurse's uniform comes into view. The woman's stern features are at odds with the look of concern he sees in her blue eyes. She motions for him to be still and smiles gently.

'Calm yourself, Herr Sterling. There is nothing to be upset about. Doctor Oglethorpe has sent for the Professor. The doctor said your stitches would heal fine and there is no sign of blood poisoning.'

'Ah, my patient is awake at last.' This voice belongs to a heavy set man in long white lab coat talking thru a bushy, brown beard beneath a red round nose and a full head of uncombed brown hair. Sterling smiles in spite of himself.

'Yes, nothing to fear, Mr. Sterling. Allow me to make the proper introductions. I am Professor Peaslee of the Boston District Bureau of Military Information's Science Division. and this is Miss Schmidt, a most capable and efficient nurse. You are Mr. Sterling, a hero or so I have been told.'

'What about Archie...Mr. Rawlings?'

'Oh, he isn't here. I believe he made his report Tuesday and is staying with a local family until his injuries are healed.'

'Ja, the woman who took care of him on the train, a Miss Construe; I believe. Her family was most insistent that the young man stay with them until he is fit for duty. I heard the two are engaged to be married.'

'OH, my. Oh, poor Reggie has outsmarted himself this time.' Sterling starts to laugh and cough at the same time and the nurse quickly administers a sedative fearing for his stitches.

Later, alone in his recovery room, Sterling awakes and once more practices with his copper, clockwork arm and its gleaming silver hand. Sterling raises his left arm and marvels at the five metal fingers on his hand. He turns his head and sees the small gears twisting at the elbow of the marvelous arm. Where Doctor Freiherr's ungainly iron appendage caused him pain in his shoulder and embarrassment with its three fingered claw; this arm is beautiful and more art than prosthetics. Sterling grasps a nearby metal tray and hears the knives and other instruments clink, but, he is already able to control the arm enough to not knock over the tray. He releases it and is surprised to see his finger's imprints in the metal. He tries to continue exercising the marvelous arm; a boyish smile on his face as he gets use to its grace and movements. He feels the first drops of sweat and the ghost of pain in his shoulder, but, he does not want to quit. It is while he is using the arm to pull himself painfully up to a sitting position that the nurse walks in.

'No, stay still. You lie still and let the sutures heal. Doctor Oglethorpe will be most cross with us both if you tear them free. The doctor spent a lot of time getting you back together properly.'

Out of the hospital and Into the Fire

It is another day of quiet exercise and bed rest for Sterling, that is, before a lovely young blonde lady comes into his room and throws a man's smoking jacket onto the bed.

'With the Superintendent's compliments, your presence has been requested upstairs.'

'Upstairs, where? Who are you?'

'Allow me to introduce myself, Lieutenant Sterling, I am Miss Sumner, Superintendent Howe's aide and an operative of the Bureau's Boston District. The superintendent has sent me to the hospital wing to collect you and bring you to his office for a meeting. Now, if you do not mind, please put on the jacket and let's be going.'

Sterling sits up and the bed sheet falls down revealing his scarred chest and the brass and copper clockwork left arm. His face turns red as he reaches out with his right hand and struggles to put the smoking jacket on. Miss Sumner walks forward and shyly helps the young man maneuver his clockwork arm into the smoking jacket's sleeve. She looks at the floor while he awkwardly pulls on his trousers and belts the jacket closed. She looks up briefly at Sterling's grass stained Union blue trousers and notices the way his hands pull on the boots unconsciously as if they are a natural part of him. Without a word, she walks out into the hall. Sterling walks steadily behind the lovely young lady, a thousand questions running thru his mind, to the end of the hallway and up a wide set of stairs.

Miss Sumner gives the heavy oak door of the Superintendent's Office a most unladylike knock and opens it at a muffled 'Come In' from the other side. She stands to the side and gives Sterling a smile and a nod beckoning him to go inside alone.

Sterling walks into the plush office with its mahogany desk and dark wood paneled walls. He looks at the balding, heavy set man sitting behind the desk and then to the room's other occupant. The medium build man wears his sergeant's uniform like it is a tuxedo without wrinkles, creased and hand pressed; only the fading blue of the wool dye gives a sign of age. The Sergeant stands on the far side of the desk smoking a cigar, the smoke curling above his bushy mustache and goatee. Sterling looks back on the Superintendent; the man behind the desk is of medium build, dressed in a charcoal gray suit and has the bearing of a man that is use to being in charge. It is the steel in his grey eyes that truly mark him as the Superintendent. The other man stares at Sterling with eyes so dark brown as to be black beneath a full head of long brown hair. The man's mustache and goatee show the first hint of gray and seem to compliment the Sergeant's weathered face and in Sterling's mind complete his unsmiling portrait.

'Mr. Sterling, I am Superintendent Howe and this gentleman is Sergeant Fitzpatrick. He will be assigned to you and will assist you with your endeavors while you are in Boston.'

'Good day, sirs, Sergeant. I am sure it is a pleasure to meet you both.'

'We owe you a debt of gratitude for saving the Analytical Engine from those train robbers. Also, Doctor Oglethorpe and Professor Peaslee were quite beside themselves when the bodies of the three iron men were brought in. I dare say you have provided them with weeks of investigation and experimentation. I'll likely hear about all sorts of esoteric wonderment in excruciating detail before they are done,' says Superintendent Howe, his mouth moving into a frown as he pictures the men's inevitable visit to his office.

'I believe they have repaid any debt owed me with this magnificent clockwork arm. I can't begin to tell you how superior it is to my old one,' says Lt. Sterling.

'Well, I believe that's enough pleasantries for now. Let's get down to business, shall we gentlemen. Mr. Sterling, I don't have any specific orders for you at the moment. Sergeant Fitzpatrick will take you to the quarters that we have arranged for you nearby in Charlestown. I believe you will find them quite satisfactory. Oh, I almost forgot. Mr. Rawlings sends his regrets that he could not wait here for you. Seems he had to return to New York rather quickly. He has accepted an immediate posting to London; quite unexpectedly I'm told.' The Superintendent looks puzzled as Sterling begins to smile widely.

'Really, I don't know of any operations going on in London, sir.' Sterling can just picture Rawling's escape from Miss Construe and a marriage proposal; the man would rather face cannon fire than actually settle down and have to lead a respectable life.

'Actually, Superintendent James credited young Mr. Rawlings with the idea of setting up a small shop to watch our English cousins. Given that we have had to fight them twice now for our independence and came very close to a third altercation after they mistakenly gave aid to the rebellious southerners, it seems prudent for the Bureau to have a presence in their country and guide them away from any future endeavors to recapture their colonies' says

Superintendent Howe with a certain harshness born of his Boston ancestors.

'Lieutenant Sterling, if you are feeling up to it, we will collect your belongings and be on our way. Let's get you out of the Superintendent's hair, no offense your lordship.' So saying, Sgt. Fitzpatrick lays a hand on Sterling's shoulder to turn him towards the door when the young man stiffens and asks an unexpected question.

'Gentlemen, what happened to the teletype I found on one of the horses? There was a message from the airship…Something about Doctor Freiherr if I remember correctly?'

'What's this about an airship? There was no mention of any of this in Mr. Rawlings' report.'

'Uh, no sir, this all happened after he was injured.' Sterling stares at the expressions on the two men's faces. The young operative from New York is certain that he has made some error of judgment or mistake judging by their shocked expressions.

The stout Superintendent runs his hand thru his thinning red hair then picks up the phone on his desk and talks quietly into it. Within a minute, the same lovely blonde haired young lady that escorted Sterling to the office enters the office carrying a silver coffee set. Sterling can not help but notice the way her hips sway beneath her flowing brown dress as she moves across the room. She sets the coffee pot and cups down on a low table and then turns around without a word. She flashes a pearly white smile at Sterling and he falls deeply into her sparkling blue eyes before she walks quietly out of the room. Sterling stands not breathing, absently holding his clockwork left arm with his flesh and blood right hand as he watches her shapely form before it disappears on the other side of the closing oak door.

The Superintendent makes a second far less cordial phone call before he and Sgt. Fitzpatrick move to the table. The two men begin talking and pouring steaming cups of coffee; motioning for Sterling to join them. Sterling is still thinking about Miss Sumner's brilliant smile and dimpled cheeks when the real de-briefing begins.

The Superintendent informs Sterling that the teletype never arrived with the crates from the train. None of the Boston guards sent to meet the train can remember seeing the saddle bag that night; presumably it is still in the box car wherever it has gotten off to. The Superintendent lets this news sink in before asking Sterling to once again recount the raid on the train and the events of that day. Sterling sips his strong coffee and tries to remember as many details as he can about the raiders and the airship seen from a far as it climbed into the night sky. He is certain only that the teletype's punched paper tape mentioned Doctor Freiherr by name. Sergeant Fitzpatrick asks a few questions regarding the remarkable iron encased raiders and how Sterling and Rawlings were able to dispatch them. At some point in the re-telling of the raid, a clerk walks in with a tray of cold chicken and milk for the men to eat.

It is sometime later before Sterling is able to leave the office. By now all his tired thoughts are centered on getting out of the office and letting his voice and brain rest. He walks out of the building with his head low on his chest following in Sergeant Fitzpatrick's footsteps. He climbs mechanically into a carriage and sinks back into the leather padding of its bench seat while Sgt. Fitzpatrick readies the steam boiler and its engine. Sterling looks out the carriage window watching as they exit the Navy Yard past armed guards and chug and clank their way along cobblestone streets before stopping in front of a fine brick row house. Sterling asks the sergeant where they are as he climbs down from the comfortable carriage's interior.

'We are at a Bureau house on Trenton Street here in Charlestown proper, sir. We own the end row house and frequently set it up for visitors. Sorry there wasn't time to engage a house keeper, but, we figured you would rather sleep in a real bed rather than going back to the hospital wing.'

The young Sterling weaves slightly as he walks behind Sergeant Fitzpatrick up to the row house's front door. He walks into the house's foyer and looks around him. The small foyer is cozy enough and only broke up by a table against the front wall and an umbrella stand complete with a black umbrella already provided.

'Sergeant, it has been an exhausting day and all I want now is to sleep; where is the bedroom?'

'Well, I was going to give you the penny tour' says Sgt. Fitzpatrick.

'I will gladly give you a two cent piece if you cut the tour and point me to a place I can sleep; oh and some proper clothes are definitely in order ' Sterling says stifling a yawn.

'Right, well. The clothes I can arrange, but, not tonight. As to sleeping, the bedroom is up these stairs first door on the right.'

Sterling walks a couple of paces to the stairway and looks up. 'That would be the only door on the right; correct?'

'Yes, sir, you did say you wanted the abbreviated tour.'

'So I did. Before you leave, I expect, from what the superintendent said that we will be leaving town tomorrow and going back to the site of the attempted train robbery?'

'Yes, sir. I will be here at sunrise to fetch you; complete with a suitable wardrobe. Not that I see a lot of promise in us spending the next few days searching for your Doctor Freiherr or the raiders. From what you said and what I read of Rawling's report, the raiders are all dead and no one saw this doctor. Airships being what they are tend not to leave tracks that you or I can follow too well on the ground.'

'I can not argue any of that, but, we do need to investigate the site and any towns nearby for clues as to where those raiders came from. And I would dearly like to find that blasted teletype machine, just for my own peace of mind. Those raiders were well supplied and their horses fresh; they couldn't have ridden very far before setting the trap for the train. Someone has to have seen them and the airship.'

'Well, if you say so, sir. We'll head north in the morning. I expect we'll start with Salem and then the section of rail tracks where the raiders hit the train. From there I guess we'll just have to see where the chase leads us.'

'Quite right. But, tonight the chase is going to lead me up these stairs and straight away to bed and to sleep. Oh, Sergeant Fitzpatrick, right?'

'Yes, Fitzpatrick.'

'I will need to impose on you for one more item. It seems my pistol is another item that did not make its way to Bureau Headquarters. I would be obliged if you could procure a replacement for me.'

'Ha, sorry, yes sir. I apologize for not thinking of that. Can't be a proper officer or Bureau operative without a proper side arm. I'll have you one pistol and holster come tomorrow morning when I return.'

'Thank you, and goodnight.'

'Goodnight to you, Lieutenant Sterling.'

The Glass Coffin

Boston's North End, Night

It is Friday night at the Elephant & Tiger Tavern deep within Boston's North End on the infamous Ann Street, a tawdry part of town well deserving of its risqué reputation as a home to Boston's most notorious taverns, brothels and cheap boarding houses. A lovely young lady with coal black hair and ruby painted lips belts out a lively Irish tune. She bounces seductively to the music in her low cut emerald green, ruffled dress. The young woman's blue eyes flash as she winks at the men in the tavern. With a swift turn, those wild blue eyes disappear behind her long bangs and wildly flowing black hair as she twirls around and jumps in time with the music. The fiddle player picks up the tempo even more and the crowd cheers. The men standing at the mahogany bar with its brass railing lift their beer mugs and sing the song heartily if not in tune. And above it all a haze of cigar smoke warms the tavern. In the center of Boston's Ann Street, the Elephant & Tiger Tavern is in full swing in the late night hours.

At a table away from the bar and the dancer, near the back wall, another lovely young woman, this one with long red hair listens to the music with a wistful smile on her full lips. She watches with sparkling green eyes as the dancer spins and the fiddler plays and taps one laced black leather boot in time to the music. The young woman doesn't seem bothered by the dim, flickering gas lamps that dimly light the tavern or the haze of cigar smoke; her eyes not missing a thing that happens in the dim tavern. The woman sits back when the band takes a break and crosses her legs; hiking her green gown a little too far to be a proper lady. She sips her red wine and tries not to show interest in the leering men at the bar.

Mr. Jim Nichols, fresh from his shift at the docks, wipes the beer from his walrus mustache and runs a dirty hand thru his greasy black hair. He screws up his courage and makes the long walk to the red headed lady's table with a beer in hand and a cigar hanging out of his mouth like a smoke stack for one of the North End's many factories. The drunkard introduces himself to the red head and is rewarded when she replies with her name; Persephone. She looks past the man at the band as it starts back to playing, but, he doesn't notice. He tries to coerce the lady into joining him at the bar; she refuses. He tries to entice her into offering him a seat at her table; she doesn't. Finally, he throws two dollar bills on the table and roughly suggests she earn the money on her back.

Nichols should flee when Persephone turns blazing sea green eyes and a cruel red rouged mouth towards him at the sight of the money and his crude suggestion, but, he is too drunk or too dull witted to recognize his mistake. Instead, he smiles widely and falls in beside her as she scoops up the money and stomps out of the tavern's rear exit.

Once in the dark alley, the heavy set man grabs Persephone roughly by the shoulders and spins her around to face him. Persephone nearly chokes on the strong odors of urine and vomit that fill the alleyway. The man pulls her in close to him. She can smell beer and cigar smoke on his reeking breath as he leans his mouth in to kiss her. She can also see the shocked look on his face and hear his skull crack as she grabs the larger man and throws him to the cobblestone covered ground of the alley. The man's wool suit soaks up the watery waste as he lies semi-conscious from the fall. She drops on top of the stunned man and a sliver of moonlight gleams off of pearl white fangs just before she dips her head and sinks those fangs deep into the man's fleshy neck.

She drinks in the blood and her eyes roll backwards as the warmth fills her body. Her senses are heightened and she can hear and smell the small vermin scurrying about in the alley. She can smell the cool, ocean saltwater of the bay and less appealing smell of the fish market beneath the ashes from the coal smoke. She keeps her eyes closed listening to the clip clop of horses pulling unseen carriages; the wagon's iron shod wooden wheels clacking along over the uneven cobblestones. Briefly, she hears the distant clanking and chugging of a steam carriage rolling somewhere in the North End. She sniffs and the fouls smells of the alley come alive to her, but, always less real than the scent of blood. All too soon, the warm blood runs out and she reluctantly raises her head. Remembering past troubles, she bites the man's neck with her whole mouth and rips a wide patch of skin and flesh from his cooling neck and spits it out to the unseen denizens of the alley. Now, she thinks, there is no telltale puncture marks to identify her prey.

She is on her way to enjoy what remains of her night; now that her evening's meal is done. She holds a handkerchief to her mouth and dabs gently at a small bit of blood before turning with a wide smile and walks casually out of the alleyway onto the street beneath the dim yellow gaslight. The young lady walks down the street past more taverns with the raucous sounds of music and men enjoying themselves and turns onto Commerce Street. With a sense of warmth and comfort that is far too fleeting, she walks out to a nearby wharf and stares at the massive hulls of the merchant ships of Boston and then up at the starry sky and the baleful moon. She wonders, fleetingly, what it would be like to sail those same ships beneath the warmth of the sun and the salty air of the sea. For just a few moments, Miss Persephone Blackstone knows peace.

Ann Street, a Body Found

Patrolman Gifford's hobnail boots ring out loudly in the early morning quiet of Boston's Ann Street as he walks along the cobblestones on his patrol. The young man looks around at the dirty red brick buildings that line the street with their soot stained windows. He can barely see the darker black smoke from the factories as it wafts up thru the morning fog. The smell of coal furnace smoke from the countless smokestacks hides the less prevalent smell of the docks and fisheries. He turns the corner and quickly steps aside into an alleyway; splashing an unhealthy amount of wet material over his black shoes as he jumps into a puddle from last night's brief cleansing rain. He shakes his pasty white fist at a chugging steam carriage as it rolls past; tiny sparks flying from iron shod wagon wheels as it rolls swiftly over the cobblestones. Patrolman Gifford gives a heartfelt opinion on ungentlemanly behavior of some drivers and is about to step back out onto the relatively clean street when a sound behind him catches his attention.

He calls out to the empty alley and steps further into the rain soaked, refuse strewn brick walkway. His sea green eyes dart left and right at the stacks of empty crates lining the walls. His hand draws his revolver; thinking this is only the second time in his police service that he has drawn his pistol while in the field. He is midway down the alley when a wooden crate to his left falls loudly to the ground splitting open. He points the revolver a little unsteadily and steps forward. Suddenly, a cat leaps from the empty space in the stacks and lands amongst the hay and remains of the crate before springing off and away. The young man holsters his pistol and raises his blue cap wiping sweat from his brow. He looks down and gets another shock as he notices a man's brown leather shoe, the foot still in it and attached to a leg, lying sideways in the muck and mud. Gifford steps closer and kicks the sole of the shoe while calling out for the vagrant to wake and leave. No movement. The young patrolman can now see the whole man laying still, his throat ripped out. The water seems to have washed away the man's blood without soaking the man himself.

The young patrolman runs out of the alley and stops at a Police Box on the corner. Gifford's hands are mostly steady as he uses a brass skeleton key to open the box and reaches for the telegraph key. He reports his grizzly find to police dispatch and tells them to send a coroner's wagon to the alley behind the Elephant & Tiger Tavern. The answering signals are converted to text on the Visual Display Unit and the constable smiles as the professional response comes back asking for a further description of the said dead body and promising to send an Orderly Wagon round straight away. Gifford replies that he found a male in his thirties lying amidst the filth of the alley dead as a stone and could the telegrapher please have someone come and take it off his hands. The patrolman smiles ruefully at the next pronouncement from the clicking telegraph; he is to stand guard over the corpse until the Orderlies arrive. What a rotten start to a rotten day.

Gifford, once again alone in the alley with his find, bends down and carefully turns the corpse's head looking for further injury or clues to his cause of death; not that a torn out throat isn't enough to kill a man.

Fifteen minutes seem like as many hours to the patrolman as he waits for the coroner wagon to arrive. He is relieved and frankly grateful for the human company when a chugging steam wagon pulls into the entranceway of the alley and two white coated Orderlies exit. One busily grabs a cloth stretcher by its wooden handles while the other walks purposely past Gifford and bends down over the body. The Orderly grunts a few times and seems to be talking to himself while writing in a small notebook. The Orderly walks up to Gifford and thrust the open notebook and an iron tipped pen at the young patrolman.

The Glass Coffin

'Patrolman, please read my description of the scene and sign if you agree to the situation and the state of the body, sir.'

Gifford glances at the incomprehensible scribbling and dutifully signs his name at the bottom of the page.

'Thanks, sir. Now, we'll be taking the body to the morgue. You can return to your patrol. There's nothing more as can be done here.'

So saying, the white uniformed orderly puts away his notepad and helps his partner load the heavyset man's corpse onto the stretcher. The orderlies are already talking about past adventures as they carry the stretcher between them to the back of the wagon. Gifford winces at the balancing act that is performed while the front orderly opens a wide metal door at the back of the wagon. The two men manage to slide the stretcher into the wagon and flop it onto a smoking bed of dry ice. The iron door closes and a wave of black smoke fills the alleyway as the wagon chugs away.

Gifford coughs waving madly at the fresh smoke. He walks back to the police box and dutifully uses the telegraph again to report the arrival of the coroner wagon and their custody of the corpse. He is about to close the box and return to walking the silent fog bound streets when the clicking begins and the screen brightens into life.

'Acknowledged patrolman Gifford, any thoughts on the cause of death?'

'Man's throat was torn out, as if by an animal. Blood evidence washed away by last night's rain storm I am not sure, but, I think we can safely rule out suicide.'

'Acknowledged, patrolman, sorry I asked.'

Gifford smiles for the first time that morning and whistles while he walks down the street.

The War Remembered

In a quiet brownstone row house in the center of
Charlestown a sleeping Lieutenant Sterling lies in sweat
soaked sheets gripped by a hauntingly realistic nightmare.
A nightmare all the worse for it is born of the truth. It is
again 1864 and the Union has Petersburg surrounded by a
line of trenches; it is a city under siege. The Union Army's
V Corps is in the field and young Lieutenant Sterling leads
a large detachment tearing up the railroad tracks breaking
the supply line of the Army of Northern Virginia.

A haze in the distance obscures the distant woods of
the countryside. Sterling sniffs the clean air so fresh after
the morning autumn rain. He smiles waving his arms,
feeling the heavy weight of his rain soaked wool uniform.
His black leather boots make an odd squishing noise as he
plows thru the puddles in the clay and dirt soil. His skin
heats up fighting the cool of the rain water as the afternoon
sun overhead tries to dry the land and his uniform. In the
distance, he can hear laughter as the soldiers use picks and
shovels to pry the iron rails loose.

Young lieutenant Sterling turns to look at a group of
soldiers rolling a section of heavy iron rail off the track and
down the small embankment. More soldiers gather it up
and manhandle it into a roaring bonfire that somehow

survived the brief rain. He turns his head away from the fire and sees shapes moving in the distant line of trees. Without thinking, he draws his cap and ball pistol and squints trying to peer deeper into the trees.

A wave of gray clad Confederate infantrymen breaks thru the tree line into the field; their voices screaming a high pitched rebel yell. Sterling stands stock still watching the white smoke rising from blue steel barrels as some of the rebels stop and fire their black powder rifles.

His pistol still drawn, Sterling turns and shouts a warning to the Union soldiers. They quickly drop their tools and pickup their rifles. He fires at the rebels more as a reflex than with any hope of actually hitting his target. Down the tracks, the sound of rifle fire is mixed with the shouts of Union soldiers as they run back towards Sterling. He quickly gives up the idea of making a stand out in the open as they are and waves the men on to the railway station.

Running towards the station with his men, Sterling sees a soldier stop and fire back at the oncoming wave of Confederates; then pitch over dead a bloom of bright red blood on his blue chest. Still more soldiers run alongside Sterling as they make their way for the railway station and its wood and earthworks revetments.

The Glass Coffin

Sterling stands behind a line of crouching Union soldiers poised behind a low wooden and earthworks wall. The soldiers fire their rifles and the air is filled with flames and smoke and the smell of burnt gunpowder. Here and there, a gray clad figure falls down; only to be replaced immediately as the Confederate soldiers continue their charge.

Sterling cocks the hammer on his .44 caliber pistol and fires his last minie ball at the screaming gray wave coming at him. He steps backwards and hastily pulls out a powder flask and starts the slow task of reloading his pistol. His eyes roll left and right while performing the rehearsed, memorized steps and he sees how the line of Union defenders has shrunk. He bites a mercury cap before placing it onto the pistol and turns at a shout from nearby. His eyes grown wide at the sight of a grinning, yellow skull that he somehow knows is his sergeant. The skull opens its jaws soundlessly as the rebel bullet strikes it in the forehead and explodes out the back sending the heavyset man heavily to the ground.

A race as the few surviving Union soldiers run from the earthworks into the railway station. Immediately, the soldiers thrust their black powder rifles thru the windows and begin shooting at the line of Confederate infantry.

Another flash of black powder flames and small clouds of smoke mark a round of rifle fire as the desperate Union soldiers try to keep the wave of gray soldiers from washing over them. Sterling tilts his head and listens to a high pitched whistling of an incoming cannon shell.

The explosion turns the railway station wall into a hornet's nest of red hot iron shrapnel and burning wood. A huge hole appears in front of Sterling and he sees a Union soldier at the window disappear; only to be replaced by a gaping hole and a clear view of the soldiers outside. He hears a familiar voice screaming in pain, but, can see no one nearby. Finally, he looks down at his left arm; its uniform shredded by shrapnel and recognizes the screaming voice as his own.

Sterling watches from above the railway station as a mass of Union blue cavalry rides into the Confederates and ends their attack. The blue uniformed horsemen fire pistols while waving sabers or fire Spencer repeating rifles into the gray clad wave and it breaks. The rebel infantrymen turn to face the new threat, but, it is too late.

Sterling, still hovering over the station looks down as his unconscious body lies in a medical wagon with other wounded men racing down a dirt road to the field hospital. Below him, at the station, less than a dozen defenders walk or limp out of the burning building while a thick fog rolls in covering everything.

Sterling lies on a wood table while a masked Doctor Freiherr works feverishly to finish stitching up his left shoulder and chest. The doctor is alone in the room with no orderlies or other physicians while he mumbles and tries to sew the flesh closed around the rounded iron that forms Sterling's left arm. Sterling looks down at the floor beside the operating table and there lies his bloody left arm hacked off and discarded.

A dark bedroom and an older version of that young officer sits up screaming; the nightmare fading with the opening of his ice blue eyes. He looks around the sparsely furnished room while his right arm reaches over and grabs the cold metal where his left arm use to be. Even now, the cylinders and gears feel slightly cold to the touch and phantomlike. Copper and brass fingers flex as the man uses both arms to propel himself out of bed. He turns up the flame on a nearby gas lamp affixed to the wall, then stretches and yawns deeply. Outside, the sun is just rising; another day has started for Lieutenant Reginald Sterling.

He holds his top hat in his left hand, mindless of the brim crushed between square metal fingers. The sandy haired six foot tall Sterling springs down the stairs of the row house with his boots thundering in the early morning quiet. On the street, an older man in a immaculate Union blue Sergeant's uniform stands already holding open the passenger door of an ornate black and gold steam carriage. The grizzled veteran tips his slouch hat in greeting to the younger man. Sterling takes a moment to admire the black carriage with its six iron rimmed wagon wheels and four black gold tipped smoke stacks rising into the sky at the back of the steam boiler and the plush carriage sitting atop the furnace that forms its undercarriage. He nods to the sergeant before he steps into the plush interior and sits on a bench seat. He turns back to the open door and asks, 'Sgt. Fitzpatrick, how is it you are waiting for me already? Tell me you didn't wait here all night instead of going home. Or is this some Bureau skullduggery set so you know just I awaken and will have need your chaperone services?'

'No mystery at all, Lieutenant Sterling. I've been paying some attention this past week during our shall we say travels. I simply timed my arrival with the rising sun and trusted that your worthiness will soon pop out of yon house eager to begin another fine day.'

Chuckling, Fitzpatrick closes the door and walks to the front of the carriage and his semi enclosed front seat with its steering wheel and gearbox. A few deft taps and the turn of the correct knobs and the steam carriage's engine cogs begin to whirl and its gears engage. The red and black painted steam carriage begins chugging along the cobblestones leaving a sooty trail of coal smoke behind it to darken the early morning fog.

As the steam driven carriage bounces, chugs and clanks its way towards the Charlestown Navy Yard, Sterling pushes his back deeper into the plush coach's cushioning and closes his eyes. A solid week spent searching for clues that would lead to the mysterious Iron Men and possibly their leader Doctor Freiherr. Long hours spent listening to survivors of the recent train robberies and their tales of iron horsemen and vampire soldiers, but, not one word mentioned by any of them about the mad doctor. The young operative found enough rumors and listened to enough witness statements to become convinced that the train robberies in the east were connected to the thwarted attempt to steal the Bureau's remarkable Analytical Engine. Sterling reflects on the days spent riding in the steam carriage between railway stations going to the small towns near the train robbery sites and finding no evidence that would lead him to the raiders' base or give him a clue about their present activities. He is still convinced that the involvement of Doctor Freiherr holds the key to some larger evil being perpetrated, but, what, he wonders. As Sterling's eyes close, his hand unconsciously curls around the butt of his new LeMat Pistol and his mind drifts back in time.

Doctor Freiherr, physician, alchemist and sawbones for the Army of the Potomac's vast medical corps. Once a great boon to the men wounded in the War Between the States, the doctor saved countless soldiers from dysentery, infection or worse. Thought during the war to be a great humanitarian; the doctor's mind hid its evil thoughts well. It was only after Doctor Freiherr was ordered to report to a hospital behind the lines and away from the battlefield that the madman's darker activities came to light.

Sterling's sleeping face twitches briefly as he recalls waking up in a proper hospital bed after his ordeal in the field hospital with a nurse checking the stitching around the young lieutenant's new steam powered iron left arm. He looks up at the angelic face of the white uniformed nurse and tries to tell her about Doctor Freiherr and his ruined arm, but, she turns and fades into the distance. A greasy dark haired steam mechanic stands to one side of the hospital bed examining the unique prosthetic limb. The engineer busies himself testing the movements of Sterling's field hospital replacement left arm while explaining to the young officer that no one has heard from Doctor Freiherr; he never returned from the field hospital. It seems there were some rumors and possible charges against the doctor brought about by some unorthodox surgeries that he had been performing. Sterling rolls his neck to the left and sees the crude rivets, gears, steam cylinders all ending with a crude metal claw. This then is his new left arm. He falls unconscious as a fresh wave of pain washes over him.

Bureau of Military Information, Boston District

'We're here, Mr. Sterling. It's time to protect the world from Democracy.' Sgt. Fitzpatrick is smiling as he opens the carriage door revealing a massive, multi-gabled red brick multi-winged monstrosity of a building. The multiple steeped roofs of the building connect with other branches and sport round towers midway on opposite sides. Sterling can't tell how many wings the huge Victorian mansion has, but, it is three stories high if it is a foot. The startled veteran officer can just make out the morning sunshine gleaming off of copper and steel from the barrels of the Gatling Guns sticking out at the tops of the building's round towers. He stretches luxuriously after his brief nap and looks at the bearded, mustached sergeant; as always carrying his Spencer Repeating Rifle this time held casually in one hand.

'Sergeant Fitzpatrick, somehow I don't think that's the proper motto for the Bureau of Military Information. What would General Grant think of our loyalty? Hang that, what would the Superintendent say? Ah, now that is a proper look of respect.'

Sterling spoils the dressing down by smirking and then laughing briefly, 'Now, it is time for me to report in to the Superintendent on the waste of a solid week looking for our mysterious train robbers. If that wasn't enough of a punishment, I am sure Professor Peaslee will ask for me to come to his laboratory so he can perform some diabolical adjustments to my new mechanical hand. So I will have quite a filling day without you. It is time for you to find some other deviltry to get yourself into. I will be sure to tell the superintendent of your invaluable service this past week. I would doubtless have been lost a hundred times if I had gone on my own into the wilds of Massachusetts. I will send word to you when I am ready to leave this evening.' Sterling snaps off a half wave, half salute at the grinning sergeant; then turns and walks towards the pair of guards standing outside the monstrous Bureau Headquarters. The young officer eagerly walks past the pair of guards standing in front of the building's main entrance. He raises a quick salute and chuckles at the soldiers' perplexed expressions as they stare at his metal hand before throwing open the heavy oak door so Sterling can walk inside.

Sergeant Fitzpatrick waits until Mr. Sterling has vanished onto the covered porch and into the building before taking off his slouch hat scratching his head. The lad isn't the usual stuffed shirt New Yorker that he is use to dealing with. This wet nurse assignment may turn out to be an enjoyable adventure after all.

His black leather boots echoing in the stairwell, Sterling wastes no time in getting himself up to the top floor and to the Superintendent's Office. He bursts into the clerks' area with its rows of desks and deskbound workers. The young man's pulse quickens and his mouth goes curiously dry when he sees Miss Sumner in a rosy pink day dress and blue bonnet partially hiding her blonde curls walking out of the Superintendent's Office towards him. He tries not to stare into her deep blue eyes; but, catches himself staring at the low cut of her dress instead. His face getting warmer by the second, Sterling tries to speak normally and not rushed.

'Miss Sumner, how very good it is to see you this fine morning.'

'Thank you, Mr. Sterling. It is good to see you, as well. I'm afraid the Superintendent is expecting you and I wouldn't want you to keep him waiting.' She replies. Her hand unconsciously grabs her wide ruffled gown a bit nervously.

'Well, I won't keep him waiting long.' He stammers. 'I saw you and well … Just wanted to say hello, as it were.' Sterling feels the heat as blood rushes to his face.

The lovely young lady smiles, looking a little puzzled as to what to do next. She steps aside and starts talking to one of the clerks; leaving Sterling free to continue the long walk to the end of the aisle and the Superintendent's dark wooden office door. Sterling tries to adjust his coat as his mind starts to imagine all the correct statements and responses he could have just made to the lovely woman; instead of what actually happened. He opens the oak office door and a deep gravelly voice pulls him out of his reverie.

'Mr. Sterling, just the man I was looking for. Come into my office, please. I am anxious to hear how your search fared. I'm sure you have fresh information that will lead to the capture of the villains who dared to try and steal the Society's property; not to mention injuring or killing quite a few gallant men; yourself included. Please tell me you haven't wasted good money and a week's worth of time looking for the source of the Iron Men.'

Sterling stands a little straighter and walks into the Superintendent's office with all the grace of a school boy who's been caught passing a note in class.

The North End Revisited

The full moon hangs low in the night sky while two shadowy figures stand locked in an embrace in the alley behind the Elephant & Tiger Tavern. Persephone lifts her head; her mind racing with the excitement of fresh blood. She lets the wool suited man's lifeless body slide down the brick wall to the ground. She spits out the mouthful of flesh from his throat as the man's body falls on his side amongst the detriment of the alleyway. The young woman turns her head as she hears the first creak of the door knob turning on the nearby back door.

Persephone flees the alley in a blur and pauses only long enough to pull up a green, ruffled hood once she is on the cobblestone street. As she nears the street corner beneath the flickering gaslight post, she hears a man and woman screaming in the alleyway behind her. She frowns, her brow furrows at her near discovery as she quickly turns the corner walking off into the fog cloaked night.

Persephone walks along the water front looking out at the harbor. Even at this late hour, there are signs of life in the darkness. She hears the men's voices and sees their movements amongst the shadows. Curious, she breaks off her wandering and follows them as they climb aboard a short horse drawn wagon and clip clop away from the wharf.

She watches the wagon as it turns onto Commercial Street and clip clops its way along the emptiness. She glides from shadow to shadow following the wagon up the street until it stops in front of a three story mercantile building. She watches with a frown as the two men climb into the back of the wagon and then unload a large sea chest and a few smaller crates. One of the men looks around him before knocking on a side entrance. He steps back as the door opens almost immediately and an older gentleman in a black suit steps outside. He waves his hooded lantern shining it briefly on the second sailor and the crates, before turning to the first man and saying something Persephone can not quite hear. The man's meaning becomes clear enough as the first man runs back to the wagon and together the sailors bring the trunk and crates into the building thru the open side entrance. A few minutes and they re-appear standing with the gentleman with the lantern. Beneath its yellow light, Persephone clearly sees the stack of Bank Notes being handed to the first sailor. With a tip of their hats and mumbled gratitude, the two sailors turn and once more climb aboard the wagon. They slowly turn the horses and head back the way they came while the other man shines the lantern around once more before disappearing back into the building.

Persephone purses her lips and rubs her cold hands together for a moment before the wagon pulls up even with her hiding place. Quick as a thought, she flies from the shadows and strikes the wagon's driver sending him off the wagon and onto the rough cobblestones. The second man looks over at her and a petite balled fist smacks him in the nose knocking him senseless. The young lady frowns and reaches inside the man's dirty wool jacket and pulls the bank notes from his waistcoat pocket. With a leap, she leaves the still moving wagon and runs down the deserted street. She pauses only when she reaches the familiar ground of Ann Street and puts the money into her handbag. While not what most people have in mind, she thinks, she did earn the money after a fashion. Doubtless, neither man will risk turning the theft into the police or raising any alarm at the loss of ill gotten gains.

A short walk later and the night's excitement is fading along with her strength. Persephone breathes deeply, inhaling the smoke from coal fires and the other less identifiable scents of the city at night while she listens to the slow rhythm of her hobnail boots on the cobblestones. She steps up onto the porch of Miss

Stewart's Boarding House and turns around looking at the east sky. She imagines she can see the hint of light as she yawns and rushes into the boarding house and into her room. She is still yawning as she sheds her clothes and climbs beneath the quilted blanket. By the time the morning's first rays hit the outside of her heavily draped windows, Persephone is in a coma like sleep.

An Early Appointment

The nightmare is still fresh in his mind as Sterling exits the cozy house early the next morning. He locks the heavy oak door with its inlaid glass half wagon wheel securely behind him before bounding hastily down the row house's short set of stairs. He adjusts his pistol's position in his shoulder holster and throws a canvas haversack onto the carriage's wide soft bench seat before jumping into the carriage himself.

'Afraid I have a change to this morning's plans, Lieutenant. Seems there was a bit of trouble again at the Elephant & Tiger Tavern last night. I have orders to collect you and get ourselves over there right away' says Sgt. Fitzpatrick.

'Bit early for a nip, but, I'm always up for a trip to the pub, Sergeant. Any chance we can catch a quick breakfast while we are there?' says Sterling hopefully.

'Sorry, sir. It seems Boston Police have found a body in the alley behind the tavern and the Bureau caught wind of something odd because they want you to investigate it before the body is swept up and taken away by the Orderlies.'

'Well, no matter; I am sure the fresh air and a change of scenery will merely improve my appetite for later. Do I dare hope you have some coffee at least in the carriage?'

'Yes, as a matter of fact, I took the liberty of setting a pot of coffee in the carriage for you before the guards informed me of the new orders.'

'Excellent, see nothing can be wrong with a day that starts with fresh air, sunshine and a steaming hot cup of coffee. Now, Sergeant, lead on to the tavern and let us see what the day has in store for us.'

Fitzpatrick mutters something most uncomplimentary about cheerful people this early in the morning before climbing into his seat at the front of the carriage and gearing up the furnace's steam. Soon, a trail of black smoke puffs into the dawn sky from the accelerating steam carriage as it chugs and clanks its way down the empty morning street. Sergeant Fitzpatrick lowers the settings on the gears and boiler pressure as the carriage rolls across the new Charlestown Bridge watching for any hint of movement the entire trip across. He lets out a heavy breath as the carriage wheels leave the bridge for solid land and he smiles as he increases the carriage's speed once again.

The steam carriage bounces lightly over the last few feet of cobblestones and has barely come to a stop beneath

the gaslight beside the tavern when Lieutenant Sterling
leaps out of the carriage interior with a heavy canvas
haversack slung over his shoulder. Patrolman Gifford
immediately moves to block the path of the newcomer; a
serious look on his young face and a stern warning on his
lips. Both are forgotten as Sterling steps in front of Gifford
holding a leather I.D case with its distinctive bronze
Society of National Security's badge. The young
patrolman looks at Sterling's icy blue eyes and the patches
of copper and brass of his left arm peeking out from
underneath his ripped coat sleeve before his gaze stops at
the sight of his silver square fingered hand.

'Good morning, Patrolman. I am Lieutenant
Reginald Sterling, an operative of the Bureau of Military
Information, come to inspect the corpse, if you don't mind'

In spite of his mild manners, the young patrolman
realizes this man is dangerous trouble. Patrolman Gifford
rubs his hands on his trouser legs and tries to stammer out a
protest. He opens his mouth and begins to deny Sterling's
entrance to the alleyway before he looks past him and sees
the gleam of morning sunlight reflecting off a steel rifle
barrel. Sgt. Fitzpatrick smiles at the perspiring youth in his
blue police uniform and waggles the Spencer Repeating
rifle's barrel back and forth. Patrolman Gifford steps to the

side in silence; his eyes following the motion of the rifle barrel. Sgt. Fitzpatrick smiles and innocently points the rifle towards the sky. Sterling for his part pretends not to notice the silent drama and marches past the young patrolman with only a small ghost of a smile on his face. He makes a mental note to thank the sergeant and have a word with him about diplomacy and getting along well with others. He catches sight of his objective and races to the body his hobnail boots echoing down the alleyway.

Sterling kneels beside the dead body of a middle aged, rotund man in a mud stained dark cotton suit and scuffed brown leather shoes. The Bureau operative reaches into his haversack and removes a leather headband with a peculiar looking brass monocle made up of a stack of brass rimmed glass lenses with spring holdings and tiny rotating gears. He fits the monocle over his left eye and adjusts the myriad of spinning gears and lens until the dead man is once more in focus; yet quite a bit closer. Sterling reaches unhesitatingly into the man's waist coat and removes a worn leather wallet; empty. He thrusts the wallet into his haversack and turns the body onto its side. Sterling slowly pans over the man's coat with the monocle and stops at a curious sight. A single red hair lies ensnared in the top button of the man's coat. Curious, the operative pulls a glass vial from the haversack and a pair of tweezers and gently plucks the hair free. The red hair drops into the glass vial and then disappears into the haversack. Sterling pulls out a small vial of coal dust and sprinkles just a bit on the man's neck and collar. Sterling sweeps some excess dust away with his hand and looks for palm prints or finger prints. Another adjustment is made to the strange monocle's many lenses and Sterling is looking deep into the wound on the man's throat. A quick sneeze and a turn of the head and suddenly Sterling sees a large piece of skin beneath the monocle's view lying in the grime beside the body. Sterling smiles and watches his oversized tweezers pickup the skin, deposit it into another glass vial before it too disappears into the haversack. He is about to return to the neck wound when a commotion at the alley's entrance grows too loud to ignore.

Sterling stands and removes the marvelous monocle. He brushes his sandy hair back absentmindedly while walking towards the entrance to the alley and the loud angry voices. He sees what can only be Boston Police's Inspector Reid, a rather large red faced man dressed in a dark blue wool suit with a black bowler hat yelling colorfully at Sergeant Fitzpatrick. Two white uniformed Orderlies stand to the side in front of their steam wagon waiting to take charge of the dead body. Sterling wonders at the scene for a moment before he notices the familiar Spencer Repeating rifle being pointed by Sgt. Fitzpatrick at the alleyway. Obviously, the grizzled veteran has decided that Sterling needed some privacy with the crime scene and is enforcing that decision by gunpoint. Sterling shakes his head, angry and grateful at the same time. The Police Inspector continues to shout, making it clear he would like the Bureau operatives gone from the scene and New England as a whole.

Sterling looks up from behind Patrolman Gifford's back and waves to Sgt. Fitzpatrick. The faithful sergeant twirls his trusty Spencer Rifle and it is suddenly gone from sight. Sterling yells a friendly greeting to police Inspector Reid. Reid turns to face this new impediment and demands that he vacate the premises and quit mucking about with legitimate police business. Sterling makes to tip his hat to the Inspector before realizing he left it in the carriage. Instead, he promises to make no more demands on the gentleman's time and to vacate his jurisdiction. So saying, Sterling calmly climbs into his steam carriage. He voices a sincere apology to the inspector and tells Fitzpatrick to convey him back to Charlestown and the Bureau's Mansion with all due haste. The carriage is almost out of sight of the stunned police officials when Sgt. Fitzpatrick begins to laugh.

A Visit to the Laboratory

Arriving at the monstrous multiple roofed, red Victorian mansion of the Boston Headquarters, Sgt. Fitzpatrick has barely stopped the steam carriage and is still adjusting the boiler's pressure when Sterling throws open the carriage door and runs for the wide staircase. The operative turns and remembers to thank the sergeant for his invaluable assistance at the alleyway and for the fine coffee before running past the shocked guards and into the building's interior. The stunned Sgt. Fitzpatrick smiles; wet nursing Sterling may turn out to be a better assignment than he thought. It is certainly proving to be entertaining.

Sterling bounds out of the stairway onto the second floor still running with the haversack held under one arm. He wastes no time knocking and instead bursts into a laboratory throwing open its oak door and closing it heavily behind him. He takes two steps into the room and promptly runs into a padded brick wall in the shape of a seven foot tall bald man. Lieutenant Sterling's face flushes red as he rebounds into the door just closed behind him. He is in the middle of a shocked apology when a laughing Professor

Peaslee walks up to the leaning Sterling and the still standing giant.

'Ah, Sterling, quite an entrance to be sure. Yuri, I believe Professor Oglethorpe would like your assistance at the back table, if you would be so kind.'

The giant of a man smiles meekly apologizing to Sterling in a deep bass voice before walking off casually to meet with Professor Oglethorpe.

'Professor Peaslee, just the man I came to see. Nice doorstop, by the way. I have brought some items from a most unsavory alleyway back of the Elephant & Tiger Tavern in Boston that I wanted you to have a look at.'

'Of course, my boy. I am always happy to assist in any way I can. I do hope you have brought me something interesting. Professor Oglethorpe and I are still enjoying your last gifts. Those iron men of yours, incredible workmanship.'

'Professor, those men were no work of mine. Ever. Anyway, I've brought you a mystery, an adult man dead from a throat wound with no visible blood to accompany it.'

'Not good losing the blood like that. Blood can give valuable insight these days with proper scientific scrutiny.'

'Sorry, professor, there really was no blood. The man's throat was torn out by some type of as yet undetermined animal with not a drop of blood to be had.'

Sterling unpacks his haversack setting the glass vials carefully on the table in front of him. He also tries to describe the throat wound and the condition of the body to Professor Peaslee. The Professor gathers up the glass vials and walks away talking to them as he heads for a large brass microscope on the window sill with a large mirror turning on a small clockwork timer to continuously catch the optimum amount of sunlight.

'Professor, I have to meet with ah, the Superintendent's assistant. Would you mind if I leave the evidence with you and check back later.'
'Certainly, Lieutenant. My new friends shall keep me busy while you are away.'

Sterling tries to straighten his coat with its ripped seams and then notices something not quite right about his waist coat. The young man almost falls as he tries to climb the stairs and brush the alleyway off his trousers at the same time. Finally, he tries to button his coat still walking up the stairs and fidgeting with the material trying to coordinate his flesh and bone fingers with the actions of his metal ones. Finally, he exits the stairway and catches sight of the well shaped bustle of Miss Sumner's burgundy dress. He watches for a moment as the lovely blonde re-ties the laces of one boot before stepping out into the hallway.

'Miss Sumner, good morning.' He runs his hand absently thru his hair before asking hurriedly. 'I don't suppose you would have any interest in accompanying me to a play this Friday night? You most likely have previous plans and I don't mean to presume on you.'

'Well, that's an odd way to ask a lady for her company, but, as it turns out. I adore the theatre. What play did you have in mind, kind sir?' Sterling knows by her grin that she is playing some game with him, but, he is too happy at not hearing the 'no' that he was expecting. 'I thought I would…That is I would appreciate the pleasure of your company at the Hollis Street Theatre to see a recent play by Charles Dickens. I believe it is called, 'No Thoroughfare: A Drama: In Five Acts'.'

'Oh, I would be delighted to accompany you. I would ask that you indulge me and allow me to meet you at the theatre, as I have errands that I need to attend to Friday that might run into the evening hours.' She looks a little guilty at this subterfuge, but, the young man isn't aware of the name Sumner and its connection to Boston's society and for now, she prefers not to add to his obvious discomfort by having him pick her up at her parent's mansion on Beacon Hill.

Sterling smiles widely and quickly agrees to meet the lovely young lady at the theatre, Friday night at 8pm. He does a quick about face and bounds back into the stairway before the woman can ask him what business brought him to the third floor to begin with. She shakes her head, smiling, and walks thru the doorway into the clerk's area and down its aisle to the Superintendent's Office; hopeful nothing will come up to spoil her rendezvous with the handsome young Sterling.

A Wolf by any Name

Sterling walks more carefully as he enters the laboratory. Seeing no sign of Yuri and confident he could not miss seeing him again if he were there, Sterling walks over to Professor Peaslee.

'Hello again, Professor; how goes the hunt?'

The professor arches his back as he walks towards Sterling blinking his eyes to readjust them. The professor waves a sheaf of papers at Sterling.

'Not good, my boy. You have left me quite a puzzle, indeed. I have contacted the supervisor at the city morgue; old colleague of mine, but, a bit on the thick side. Of course, that makes him a perfect administrator. His coroner, a most gloomy sort, found no blood traces on the dead man's clothing and precious little of the fluid in the body at all. The man would appear to have been knocked to his knees and then his throat bitten and ripped out by a large animal judging from the wound's size. This is very odd behavior for any animal. Now, we have a beast that has somehow made its way to the city's North End unseen and having killed its prey leaves it to rot before disappearing again. Highly suspicious behavior. Not to mention the beast would have to be strong enough to knock a grown man down. It would have to be fast enough that the man had no time to defend himself. Then, it would have to be feral enough to bite a goodly bit out of the man's neck, but, restrained enough not feed on any part of the corpse. This is very curious indeed. I can only surmise from what you have given me that we have a rabid wolf of some kind. Now, while all that is a mystery, the red hair is less so. The hair in general matches samples we have on file of human hair and is not from the animal. No doubt the hair is a contamination from the man's misspent time in the tavern and not related to the animal attack at all.'

'So, we have a large invisible insane wolf stalking Ann Street. It has seen stranger sights, or so I've heard.'

'Oh, you haven't been listening to Fitzpatrick's tales, have you? I swear that man's adventures get stranger with each telling. Not that he isn't an excellent soldier and a top notch engineer; just I wouldn't always believe everything he tells you, if I was you.'

'Now I wouldn't rule out a large, rabid wolf for the killer. Unfortunately, the man's lack of bodily fluids is still a mystery that I can not begin to fathom. I dare say the computers even with the help of the new Analytical Engine won't be able to solve that mystery anytime soon.'

'Well, Professor, you have certainly given me enough for a start. I can look for animal tracks if the alleyway hasn't been trampled already by the Orderlies, the police and the rats that are its normal denizens. I also know that there is a red headed woman out there who might have been one of the last people to see the victim alive. Thank you very much for your time and keen insights, Professor.'

'Not so fast Lieutenant, as long as you are here there are some adjustments that Professor Oglethorpe and I would like to make to your arm. We believe we have found just the mainspring needed to increase your strength and provide for a more sustained range of motion.'

Lieutenant Sterling's groan and softer sigh can be heard clearly thru the laboratory as Professor Peaslee escorts him to a nearby table and a smiling Professor Oglethorpe comes out of some corner of the room already wheeling a table of instruments towards the two men.

A Week Gone By

Sterling returns to his house earlier than normal Friday afternoon and readies himself for his night at the theatre with the lovely Miss Sumner. He wonders for a second on the lack of sightings of a wolf or on the fact that no more murders have occurred for a week now. Well, at least no murders involving a wolf ripping out the victim's neck. He frowns and tries to comb his blonde hair into order and begins changing his clothes. He dresses for a proper night out with a brand new black top hat, wide collared white shirt with its left sleeve ripped off. Sterling frowns again as he flexes his left arm and begins to consider his appearance. He takes his time tying the wide tie and being very careful as his puts in the fake diamond tie pin. Finally he wriggles into a new tuxedo jacket with tails; closing his eyes as he thrusts his left arm into the jacket to the sound of seams tearing. His only personal item that is not brand new and that fits him properly is a 5 shot revolver hidden in the small of his back. With his new clothes smoothed repeatedly and no visible wrinkles present, the young man walks outside his row house and hails a passing hansom cab.

'The Hollis Street Theatre, please.' Sterling says to the cab's driver. The cabby tips his hat; any reply made is unintelligible beneath the man's thick scarf.

The horse's rhythmic clip clop down the streets of the strange city relaxes Sterling and he begins to grow too comfortable in the blue velvet plush seat of the horse drawn carriage. He makes himself sit up straight with an effort and tries not to wrinkle any part of his unfamiliar clothes; desperate to make a good showing of himself tonight.

Sterling arrives in front of the white marble faced theatre and exits the cab. He steps forward and stops dead in his tracks. He looks at Miss Sumner and feels the heat from a blush coming on; she is radiant. He stands mutely admiring her smiling face with its touches of rouge as she teases him by twirling around in her pearl white flowing formal gown with its wide ruffles. His mouth goes dry as he stares at her golden curled tresses flowing down the back of her dress. The young lady walks up to him and in a most unladylike manner hugs him to her. Her handbag smacks him accidentally and he smiles as he feels the hard metal of a derringer and thin bladed knife inside it. He runs his hand thru his hair absent mindedly and suddenly remembers; he left his top hat in the carriage. The young man surprises his companion by rushing away from her and running into the street. He looks frantically up the street for the horse and carriage of his cab; no hope for it the hansom cab is gone with his brand new top hat.

'Well, I've never had that reaction before. What's gotten into you, Lieutenant Sterling?'

'My sincerest apologies, Miss Sumner. I left my blasted top hat inside the carriage and now the thing's gone.'

'Oh, my. I just assumed you didn't wear one. You know, from what I have seen of you; you don't wear a hat very often.'

'That's the problem. I wear them all the time and I leave them all the time. That was the only top hat I own. It is also the third hat that I have lost since coming to this city.'

The young lady's nose crinkles up as she tries not to laugh. She gives up the battle and a melodious giggle fills the night air. Her blue eyes sparkle and Sterling laughs in spite of himself. The two stand in the street laughing as an older couple exits their horse drawn carriage and walk up to them.

A distinguished gentleman with gray mutton chops and a walrus mustache walks up to the pair with his wife holding onto his tuxedo clad arm. The older lady, in a blue

173 -The Glass Coffin

hoop skirt with a bustle, walks right up to Miss Sumner and ignoring her escort, remarks, 'Millicent, darling. How nice to see you attending the theatre again. Pass on my warmest regards to your mother and father, please.'

'Miss Arbuckle, thank you. I trust you and Mr. Arbuckle are doing well? I will be sure to mention you to my parents when next I see them.'

A smirking Sterling watches the older couple walk off, before blurting 'Millicent?'

The young blonde's face becomes stern and her tiny nose twitches, 'Not another word, Lieutenant Sterling or this evening is over. That name is to be considered a state secret; do you understand?'

A blush of red covers his face as Sterling tries unsuccessfully to wipe the smile from his face and dim the light in his eyes.

'Oh, yes. I mean, it's a very beautiful name. It so goes with all of your adventuring and the Bureau's glamorous activities. Millicent, come into my office. Millicent, there is a dangerous situation in New York and we must needs send you at once. Millicent... Ouch!'

'There. Did you get that out of your system or do I strike you again?'

'No, no more elbows; I am quite done.'

'Good, now how about you properly escort me into the theatre and let's see how well you behave in polite society.'

'Bad news, there Milli…my dear. I have never been in polite society.'

Sterling puts out his arm and the smirking blonde puts her arm in his and they walk very stately into the theatre entrance and up the stairs to their balcony seats. They are still smiling, Sterling holding Millicent's hand discretely, when the curtain goes up.

A Stroll Interrupted

Persephone looks up at the cloudy sky hiding a dim moon. She wanders the streets of North End for hours just enjoying the night; not noticing the smog or the soot that has fallen on the streets. She is hungry again, but, tries to ignore it like she has for the past few nights. She has almost a routine now for her walk and unconsciously walks past the Elephant & Tiger Tavern. She becomes vaguely aware of the alert glances of the men outside the tavern on the street. She reaches out with her senses and can barely discern the voices of men hidden in the alleyway. She walks a little quicker past the tavern and down the street. She can see shadows move under the gaslight post on the other block. She keeps walking for blocks before stopping in front of a well lit house full of music, raucous noises and laughter. She stands outside soaking up the pleasant sounds, when a young man comes up to her and thrusts a five dollar note in her face. She smiles demurely and asks his intentions. He grins stupidly and points to the Madame Tussaud's Home for Wayward Girls sign on the house with all the music and laughter coming from it. Oh, not a boarding house like Miss Stewart's; she realizes, no not at all. She laughs at her naïve notions; then shakes her head at her ignorance. She turns and gives the young man a leering look; amazed at her good fortune. The hunger has come on her and is too loud to ignore. She allows the anxious young man to guide her onto a walkway beside the house and around to its secluded back lawn. Yes, quite nice and quiet, she thinks. Persephone sits on a wooden bench and giggles quite genuinely as the handsome young man accidentally bump into her trying to sit beside her and gives her a quick kiss. She absently puts the five dollar note into her handbag before she turns on the young man. His face lights up with joy as she nuzzles his neck fondly; then turns to surprise and finally to horror as her fangs brush his whiskerless soft skin before sinking deep into his jugular vein.

Persephone stands up, smoothes out her gown and walks back onto the street with just a single sad glance back at her latest suitor. The laughter inside the house and its loud music seem to mock her solitary exile as she walks steadily back towards the boarding house. She is once more eager to be alone under the moonlight while she can.

It is in this wistful mood that Persephone rounds the corner blocks away and almost walks into the arms of a pair of heavyset men stinking of whiskey and poor hygiene. She backs away, but, the men clumsily paw at her trying to catch hold of her. She runs a short distance away in startled fear before anger asserts itself. Why is it that she can not be allowed to walk the streets unmolested? Surely, she should not have to fear what men would do to her. She turns around and walks steadily, heavy footed back down the street. The men, drunk but not stupid slow their steps for a moment at the lady's change in tactics and demeanor. They are still trying to figure out her behavior and a proper response when Persephone walks past them and turns the corner out of their sight. The two men consider following her, but, one of the men pulls a half empty whiskey bottle out of thin air or the deep pockets of his greatcoat and they continue their stroll through the city instead.

A few more street corners distant and Persephone encounters a middle aged man carrying an axe handle. The man leaps from a dark alley and demands the young lady hand over her handbag.

"Yer ladyship shouldn't be out awalking on these streets alone this late at night.' He smiles crookedly and bounces the axe handle off the calloused palm of his hand.

'Far too many undesirable elements out this time of night; no telling the dangers a lovely young lady can find herself in.' Still smiling his toothy, yellow grin, the man steps forward into the dim light and bars Persephone's path past the alley. He looks her up and down trying to picture who she is and why she is alone walking these streets. Possibly a prostitute new to the area and far out of place; or a runaway, he thinks.

'Now Missy, pardon me being so bold, but, for a small fee I can safeguard yer passage thru these dangerous streets at least as far as around yon corner.' He stops bouncing the axe handle and his dark eyes become serious and sinister as he voices his offer of assistance.

Persephone stands mute. Her mind again whirls with fear of yet another strange man out to harm her tonight; then, the beast surfaces and the anger warms her blood. Ah blood, she thinks. The young lady never opens her mouth or utters a word; even her frowning expression stays frozen on her face; her arms however move with the speed of quicksilver. The thug never quite sees the slender wrists or the delicate fingers; he sees only the small fist as it fills his vision before striking him hard on the nose. Blood spurts from the broken nose and Persephone twirls gracefully closing with the man and swooping him into a dark embrace. She steps forward and he slides back into the darkness of the alley. His eyes are still out of focus from the blow to his nose when Persephone's bone white fangs pierce his dirty neck and the blood begins to rush out of him.

Persephone steps back and the man's body falls heavily to the cobblestones. She blinks her eyes twice, shakes her head side to side and as she comes to her senses again looks down at the body. She bends down and uses a knife from his belt to tear off the flesh of his neck and throw it and the knife far into the alley's darkness. The knife falls into the muck and decaying organics of the alley as the patch of skin and its two holes sails off into oblivion.

Persephone hurries away cursing softly to herself. She walks fast down the street far from her heavily draped bedroom and safety. Her earlier mood forgotten, she races back to the boarding house and shelter from the coming sunrise.

- 180 - **Charles Reeves**

Madame Tussaud

Lieutenant Sterling runs out of the Bureau Headquarters flying out of the heavy oak doors and past the startled guards. The Union soldiers posted on the wrap around porch raise their rifles in reaction to the commotion as the young man runs down the wide stone staircase shouting.

'Sergeant Fitzpatrick! Ready the steam carriage. There's been another murder by the beast' says Lt. Sterling.

A greasy, sweating Fitzpatrick exits a nearby barn shaped wood building wiping his hands on a square piece of cotton cloth and cursing under his breath. He looks over at the young Sterling.

'What's this about leaving? I only just got the rear wheels off the carriage. Why are we off so soon?'

'The Superintendent just informed me that Communications intercepted a teletype message to Boston Police Department that a body has been found at a place name of Madame Tussaud's House for Wayward Girls. The body has a fatal neck wound and no blood was found at the scene. Now, I will be more than accommodating in going back upstairs and informing the Superintendent that you have dismantled our only transportation and that you do not feel we can leave until your repairs are done.'

'No, that will not be necessary. Ungrateful New York upstart.' The last is said under his breath even as the sergeant is turning away from Sterling and walking towards a second one story barn like building.

'Pardon me, what was that last part? I'm sure I did not hear it.' Sterling's face is positively flush from holding in his laughter. The chance for adventure is paling beside the consternation that he is causing the usually unflappable sergeant.

Sterling stands watching the grizzled veteran stomp into the barn like building. He turns back towards the headquarters and spins back around at the sound of an explosion. The young lieutenant draws his pistol and crouches down looking for the source of the loud explosion and then stands dumbfounded as an iron box on four foot high cast iron wagon wheels rolls out of the barn towards him trailing black smoke from its twin pipes mounted on the rear of the riveted box. He watches a little anxiously as the strange vehicle crosses the lawn and an iron blister at the front of the box lifts up on unseen hinges to reveal a smiling Sergeant Fitzpatrick.

'What do you think of her? I am thinking of calling it the Armored personnel engine. It's not quite finished; more of a spare time project, I suppose you would say.

However, if you are set to leave right away, now's as good a time as any to test her out.'

'Ah, quite. Tell me there is someway for me to enter that thing and that I do not have to mount it like some iron horse and ride on top.'

Two Boston patrolman stand flat footed as a monstrous eight foot long iron box clatters its way down Salem Street towards them. The men look at each other and draw their pistols; not quite knowing what else to do. They risk a quick look towards the nearby four story Victorian and consider running into its back garden for help, but, dismiss the idea just as quickly. Meanwhile, the iron carriage rolls on its wide cast iron wheels to a stop in front of Madame Tussaud's Home for Wayward Girls in a final belch of black smoke. A section of metal between the two wheels falls forward revealing a wooden staircase and two men climb out of the vehicle already deep in conversation.

'I can see the advantage of an iron covering over good wood and will agree the armor would be valuable on a battlefield, but, carriages even horses are more comfortable than riding in the belly of this beast. I am sorry, sergeant, I just cannot see such an iron coffin becoming practical.' Sterling stands bending his back to stretch out then slings the haversack over his shoulder.

'Well, lieutenant, I maintain that my Armored personnel engine is a good beast; obviously I am not finished with her design. Can you not picture riding thru a battlefield charging the enemy's line without having to worry about cannon fire or even those devilish hand grenades that the airship boys came up with just before the end. I tell you, this would put an end to infantry digging in and cannon's mowing down our lads as they cross the open ground.'

'You two, stop where you are! This is a crime scene, no one is allowed here until Boston Police personnel clear this area.'

'That's right, you need to be leaving and taking that contraption with you. The house is off limits by order of Inspector Reid.'

Sterling looks over at the two uniformed policemen for the first time; while Fitzpatrick is already pulling his Spencer rifle from within the armored personnel engine's dark confines. Sterling smoothes out his charcoal gray suit and straightens his wide black tie before announcing.

'Inspector Reid did you say, is he on the premises? The good inspector is a recent acquaintance of mine and I am quite certain he will want to see us immediately. You can be assured that the sergeant and I will be quite unobtrusive during your investigation. The good inspector will hardly know we are there.'

The distinctive metallic clicks of pistol hammers being drawn back on the patrolmen's pistols is their only reply. Sergeant Fitzpatrick makes to raise his rifle to his shoulder and Sterling reaches for his holstered pistol.

'Well, now isn't this turning out to be a fine morning' says Sergeant Fitzpatrick.

'Patrolmen, I am going to make a suggestion to you both that you really should pay attention to. Either you allow us entry to the premises and take your objections to Police Inspector Reid or you continue to enforce your objections at gun point and prepare to meet your Divine Maker. Know you both, that your last actions on this mortal plane being that you drew down on two Operatives of the Bureau of Military Information preventing them from exercising their lawful duties' says Sterling.

'Aye, lads. Listen to the good lieutenant carefully. I cannot guarantee that you both will see the Pearly Gates, but, I can most earnestly assure you that I will see you both dead and gone in some direction up or down before I fall to the ground myself.' So saying, the sergeant pulls the Spencer Rifle in tight to his shoulder.

'OH, thank goodness. You must be Inspector Reid's superior come to sort out this mess. Come with me, quickly gentlemen. You simply must convince that man to listen to reason.'

'What?'

All four men stand stunned as a young lady with raven black hair suddenly appears next to Sterling and grabbing his arm twirls him around and starts up the stairs for the house. The patrolmen look at her petticoats and long hair flowing down her back. Sergeant Fitzpatrick watches her as she skips up the stairs towing Sterling by his arm and the quickly follows the young couple lest he be left on the street to face the police alone.

Sterling crosses the entrance into the house inhaling the young woman's perfume and subtler scent of soap; his head spinning even as he tries to keep up with her. Feeling like a man caught up in a tornado, he risks a glance behind him and sees Fitzpatrick slam the heavy door closed behind them. They are all three inside the foyer and the patrolmen still standing pistols drawn out on the street staring up at the house's front door.

'Who are you two and why were those policemen about to shoot you down?' The woman is hastily wrapping a heavy dressing gown around her slender frame and pauses to pull her trapped hair from within the gown and let it fall once more across her back.

'But, you said you thought we were policemen ourselves; you know Inspector Reid's superiors.' Sterling's face is a study in fast moving confusion and observation as he looks about him at his surroundings while trying to catch up with events.

'I said that to keep them from shooting you. Also why I went out half naked in just my night clothes trying to save you two. Now, how about one of you tells me the truth. You, you look like you've been around the world a bit more; what gives?'

'Young miss, first may I introduce myself. I am Sergeant Fitzpatrick and my rather out of breath colleague is Lieutenant Sterling; we are both of the Bureau of Military Information. What you so poignantly and brilliantly interrupted was a small matter of jurisdiction and police policy.'

'Oh, I don't think I've ever seen policy at the end of a gun before. And my name is Colleen. Thanks for compliment; it was a rather witty thing to do on the spur of the moment, as it were.'

Sterling walks into the large Sitting Room staring around him at the plush velvet covered couches and handsome overstuffed chairs that fill the room. He finally stops in front of the large fireplace and rubs his hands in front of it; to stop them from shaking now that the danger has passed.

'Is this where they found the body, Miss?'

'What? Oh, no. The gentleman, well boy really was found out back in the garden on one of the benches. Stone cold dead and not a drop of blood in him; at least that's what the Orderlies said when they hoisted him onto their stretcher.'

'Well, then. Please lead us to this bench, if you would be so kind.' Says Sterling.

'What about the police out back and that Inspector Reid person? I would hate to see you two shot after I went thru such a fuss to save you?'

'Don't you fret about that, Miss Colleen. We were surprised out front. I do not believe the lieutenant or I are going to allow that to happen again. Are we lieutenant?'

'Most assuredly not, sergeant. Miss Colleen, I am most grateful for your intervention, but, believe me the lives you saved belong to those two patrolmen out front, not we.'

'All right then. I know, I'll take you to Madame Tussaud. Maybe you can make that vile Inspector cease harassing the girls and start looking for the murdering son of a whore what was here last night.'

Having made up her mind in that instant, Colleen turns on one shapely heel and starts walking for the rear of the hallway with Sterling and Fitzpatrick in tow. The scene that greets them as they walk down the back steps from the silence of the house is one of chaos and noise.

A heavyset older woman stands wagging her bejeweled finger at a uniformed patrolman shouting that she wants police protection around the clock until the fiend is caught. The young patrolman's stammering replies are lost beneath the volume of her insistence that as a citizen of Boston she is demanding and is entitled to police protection.

Further away from the house two young ladies in thin gowns and threadbare petticoats hover over another young patrolman as he walks the perimeter of the lawn inspecting the shrubbery for clues. Judging by the girls' laughter and the patrolman's blush; he is not having much success this morning. Sterling turns his head at a tap on his

189 -The Glass Coffin

shoulder from Fitzpatrick and sees Inspector Reid talking to a blond haired patrolman standing near a wrought iron bench secluded amongst the flower beds and sitting beneath a pink blossoming magnolia tree.

The two men walk steadily behind Colleen and finally are introduced to the heavyset woman as she finally runs out of steam berating the patrolman. Colleen hastily explains that the two gentlemen are not police and not friends of Inspector Reid's. Two facts that bring a smile to the Madame's face.

'Gentlemen, welcome to Madame Tussaud's Home for Wayward Girls. It is a pity it has to be under such dire circumstances that we meet, but, such is life. Now, in what possible way can I help you two and by help you I mean to cause pain or injury to that insufferable excuse for a man, Inspector Reid?'

'It is a pleasure to meet you, Madame Tussaud. I am not familiar with your establishment, but, I must say the building itself is quite magnificent. We are here merely to observe and investigate; we have no authority over the police.' Says Sterling.

'What my young comrade in arms means is that we would be happy to do whatever we can to solve this mystery and return this lovely establishment to its normal routine.' Says Fitzpatrick. He smiles widely and begins to ask the woman to show him the grounds while waving behind his back for Sterling to head for the now deserted bench; the Inspector and his patrolman now standing at the entrance to the back gardens no doubt talking to at least one of the patrolman from out front.

'

Sterling immediately heads across the lawn grateful for the chance at escape. He looks at the pink and white flower petals on the grass and takes a careful look along the ironwork of the bench before putting on his magnifying monocle looking for any clues to the murder or murderer.

Inspector Reid is about to charge over to the meddling Bureau operatives and have them forcibly removed from the premises. Watching Madame Tussaud lead the older man towards the rear of the gardens, Inspector Reid grins evilly and decides the Bureau men have a purpose in Boston after all. He sends one of the patrolmen back to police headquarters with orders to write up everything that was said or done out front; especially anything that could be presented as a threat to the patrolmen.

While Fitzpatrick is conversing with the formidable Madame Tussaud,, a second call comes over the police teletype informing Inspector Reid that a second body has been found in an alley entrance seven blocks away; a body in an unusual state. Inspector Reid gratefully and discretely leaves the lawn only pausing long enough to order Patrolman Andrews once again to stay at the scene.

Sterling finds a few drops of blood on the wooden bench. He turns at the sound of a giggle and comes face to face with white alabaster skin filling the sight of his monocle. He lifts the monocle and opens his other eye and now sees the young lady's mostly bare chest. The young man looks farther up as he straightens his back and is rewarded with a smiling brown eyed beauty with her hand absently twisting her long brown hair. The young woman giggles again and asks him who broke his goggles.

Sterling smiles and introduces himself. The young woman introduces herself as 'Julie' and asks him if he will keep her safe from the beastly murders that are occurring in the North End. The young man swells up and promises no harm will come to such a lovely creature. My god, he thinks, I sound like Rawlings. He huffs and turns back to the bench, lowering the blessedly restricting vision of the monocle and scrapes the blood into a small glass tube. He steps forward and searches for anything not wrapped in a dressing gown or wearing petticoats.

Sterling's vision is rewarded by the sight of a long strand of red hair mostly hidden by the grass beside the bench. Most curious, he thinks. He closes the eye behind the monocle and looks up at the fair haired young lady; no Julie is certainly no red haired vixen. He opens his eye and retrieves a pair of tweezers from his haversack; trying not to notice Julie's bosom as she stands bent far forward looking at the ground beside him. The young man coughs and bends down to pickup the hair and hastily put it into another glass tube. He reaches up and takes off the monocle and stows it in the haversack as well. The young woman slides uncomfortably close and asks what else he has hidden in the haversack. Quickly deciding that he needs male company, Sterling politely thanks her for her interest and makes his apologies that he is needed elsewhere. He walks away from the bench towards the relative safety of Madame Tussaud and Sergeant Fitzpatrick. He scans the garden area; two blond haired young ladies now wistful and alone at the back shrubbery. He spots a buxom young brunette standing by herself at the rear entrance of the house. Madame Tussaud with her hand entwined in her graying saddle brown hair and finally, the raven black haired Colleen standing beside the sergeant deep in conversation. For a moment, Sterling pictures Miss Sumner walking across the green grass in her night clothes; then, shakes his head and sees the flaxen haired Julie advancing towards him. A quick cough and he turns towards safety and walks steadily towards Sergeant Fitzpatrick and away from the advancing Julie.

Meanwhile, Inspector Reid has made his escape from the scene and is galloping towards the newly found crime scene. He mounts his horse and orders one of the patrolmen to use the corner police box to dispatch an Orderly Wagon to the alley where the second body has been found and promises merry hell should he arrive there and find any bureau of Military Information personnel on the premises.

In the back lawn, Sterling and Fitzpatrick busy themselves looking for more clues and ignoring the group of young women, not at all girls, walking amongst the flowers and trees of the back lawn. Neither man can help noticing the young ladies lack of modesty or proper clothing. Sergeant Fitzpatrick grins and stifles a chuckle at Sterling's obvious discomfort. Thinking on the intelligent and all too comely

Colleen, the veteran sergeant also decides that today will
not be the last time he calls on this house; one must do
what he can to help out these unfortunate young ladies, he
thinks cheerfully.

Lieutenant Sterling smiles gratefully after
Fitzpatrick makes their excuses to Madame Tussaud and a
disheartened Julie then guides him off the back lawn and
back out to the street. Neither man notices the absence of
Inspector Reid or the patrolmen out front; both lost in their
own thoughts. Sterling smiles as he climbs into the
Armored personnel engine; Boston is a most interesting
city, he thinks. The young man thinks of Miss Sumner and
her smiling face graces Julie's scantily clad figure again;
the young man quickly banishes such thoughts. He turns
and looks over at the curious controls than run along the
front of the iron box and tries to ignore the heat from the
furnace at the far end of the enclosure. He looks enviously
at the sergeant's seat with its blister top open to the
morning air. He is almost sure he hears Fitzpatrick's gruff
voice saying goodbye to the audacious Colleen before the
steam pressure warms up enough and sends the iron
Armored personnel engine clattering along the cobblestone
street and away. A red hair found at both murder scenes; a

coincidence or is the wolf's leash being held by a fiery haired master or mistress, he wonders.

Caught

The next night, Persephone is wandering aimlessly; the hunger for once not pounding in her chest and head. The young red headed woman walks further from her boarding house room than ever before, not daring to go to the tavern or back along the winding trail to the curious boarding house. Gradually she notices an improvement in the style and condition of the buildings around her. She smiles as a young couple walks past arm in arm. The man even tips his hat to her in passing.

She is still walking aimlessly when she passes a man standing beside an ornate horse drawn carriage eyeing all views of the street at once. Judging from his broad shoulders, deep chest and flinty steel eyes, the man is someone's guard, no doubt paid to stand and wait his master's pleasure. Persephone's eyes flicker to the wide stone stairway of a four story ornately decorated red brick building to her left side. She notices another hulking almost gentleman standing in front of the building's entrance at the top of the wide stairway. She hurries on anxious not to draw the attention of these particular men.

She almost succeeds, when the man at the top of the stairs opens the door to let a loud and obviously drunken gentleman out of the club house. The skinny gentleman tries to adjust his top hat and his cravat at the same time; then laughs and seems to glide bonelessly down the steps and into a waiting carriage.

Persephone is suddenly passed by the carriage and the man inside it yells for the driver to stop. The foppish aristocrat leans out the carriage window and invites the woman to ride home in safety with him. Persephone declines and turns around, suddenly eager to be back in her familiar part of town and inside her room safely at Miss Stewart's boarding house. The carriage goes on a little further and then turns around and again passes Persephone. She walks another block with the carriage pacing behind her before she turns and accepts the skinny drunkard's invitation into the carriage's black interior. The aristocrat yells for the driver to head for the Elephant & Tiger Tavern and the carriage is off into the night.

Inside, Persephone fends off the man's clumsy advances while watching the houses roll past gradually becoming more run down and dirty the closer she comes to her destination. She waits until she recognizes the neighborhood and knows her position well and true; then turns on the unsuspecting gentleman. She stops resisting his groping hands and instead draws closer to him. She braces for the pain as her fangs grow longer. She bends the man's neck away from her even as she leans her head forward. A moment and it is done and she is alive with the warmth and tingling of fresh blood. She jumps from the moving carriage and lights gracefully on the cobblestone street. The carriage driver stops the horses in alarm at her sudden departure and yells at her. The manservant jumps down from his perch and throws open the carriage door intending on chastising his master for throwing the poor wench out on the cold street. He freezes at the sight of the smallish man lying on the bench seat; his throat clearly punctured. His face drained of all color and warmth. The shocked bodyguard turns and again yells for the woman to return, but, with a different concern in his mind.

Persephone starts to run at the sound of the man's shout for her to come back. No doubt the fate of his poor gentleman employer has been found out. She expects a chase, but, the bullet that whips past her head is a new phenomenon. She spins around to see the manservant running and pointing a large revolver at her. He fires a second time from a half a block away and only her quick drop to the cobblestones keeps her from being perforated by the bullet. The young woman's green eyes go wild with genuine fear and uncertainty. She pushes off the ground with feet and hands leaping into the air and immediately running upon landing solidly on the cobblestones again. A third shot not so closely aimed brings the sound of boots and shouts from another street. She turns away from the new shouts at the intersection and runs for her life.

Patrolman Gaines blows loudly on the police whistle while running down the street, as another gunshot thunders into the night. He pauses at the street's intersection to catch his breath and spots the shadowy figure of a man up ahead. The figure fires his pistol; no mistaking that flash of gunpowder or the sound. The gunfire lights up the dim street in a flash of violence and noise. The out of breath patrolman crosses the intersection with a burst of speed intent on catching the shadowy figure when a red and black steam carriage races around the corner behind him then passes him; dousing him in a coal black smoke storm.

Sterling fires a warning shot as the carriage thunders past the still running gunman and continues on up the street intent on saving the poor fleeing female from her gun wielding assailant. He is still looking back at the brutish gunman when Fitzpatrick slows the steam carriage down and angles it to cut across Persephone's path. Sterling leaps from the carriage in front of the beautiful young woman; intent on taking her to safety when she grabs him with two dainty hands and throws him back into the side of the carriage before turning on her heels and running around the carriage's bulk and back into a headlong flight up the dimly lit street.

Sergeant Fitzpatrick smiles, no rescuing of damsels in today's society, he thinks. He watches amused as the good Lieutenant Sterling springs back to his feet and pursues the lady bound and determined to rescue her in spite of herself. He looks behind the carriage and is happy to see the patrolman seems to have the gunman well in hand.

Sterling shouts for the young lady to stop that she is safe. She turns wide eyed to look at him and demands he leave her in peace. He gains slightly on her and then is amazed as she stumbles and falls to the street in a heap. Behind him, the sun is just peaking out above the horizon. Sterling reaches down and cradles the young woman gently trying to console her and determine if she is shot and where she is injured. Persephone looks up with dull green eyes the color of dark emeralds and whispers 'Doctor Freiherr was correct; there is no defense against the rising of the sun.'

Did he hear correctly, Sterling wonders; did this woman somehow know Doctor Freiherr? If so, then how and who is she, he wonders. Sterling quickly picks up her slender form and races to meet Fitzpatrick, already coming up the street at the helm of the chugging behemoth carriage. Sterling throws the unconscious woman into the carriage and yells for the Sergeant to take them to the Bureau immediately. Sterling smiles at the unconscious young lady lying on the seat and brushes her thick red tresses away from her alabaster, attractive but oddly cold face. Even asleep, Persephone stirs something in Sterling and it is only his love of Millicent that breaks the vampire's seductive spell. Shaking his head, as if coming awake from a dream, Sterling thinks, 'Well, won't Professor Peaslee be surprised' when he brings this jewel in.

Repercussions

The next morning, a subdued Inspector Reid stands in front of the Boston Police Department's Commissioner's desk. The policeman tries not to move as listens to the older, stern faced man in enraged silence. He can't believe that his report has met with such a reaction or that he has been called before the 'Old Man' to explain himself like he was a lowly rookie patrolman. The inspector dutifully looks more attentive as his superior begins a fresh tirade.

'I'm afraid, sir, that you are mistaken. Certain members of the Office for Strategic Services did not detain a female last night after she murdered one honorable Charles Smithers. You are correct in that his manservant did engage in unlawful gunplay, but, I have been assured that no Bureau of Military Information personnel returned fire nor did they witness the man chasing an unidentified female. Now, it seems to me that you have two cases to wrap up. First there is the matter of James who I am quite sure had something nefarious on his mind and quite possibly was the instrument of his associate's death. There is also the matter of Mr. Smithers' manservant's apparent mental break down that caused him to murder his master and fire his pistol with wild abandon on our streets.'

'But, sir, I don't think that is how it actually happened. And what of the other bodies found with their throats ripped out?'

'I dare say that they will somehow be connected to the unsavory characters that we already have in custody and that their detainment will end this ghastly affair quite nicely all around. Good job inspector.'

'Yes, Superintendent. But, what of the interference of this Bureau of Military Information. Their Lieutenant Sterling and his rude partner Sergeant Fitzpatrick contaminated most of my crime scenes. I have no doubt that those two are hip deep in whatever has been going on in North End.'

'No, I repeat most assuredly, No sir. The Bureau of Military Information has not played an active part in any investigation. You do not know the names of any Bureau operatives operating in Boston. In fact, if there is any member of the Bureau called Sterling or Fitzpatrick, they have not and will not be connected with this so called 'Ripper' case. They were never in North End and you have never laid eyes on either one of those gentlemen. DO I make myself clear?'

'Quite. Yes, sir you are quite clear and I think this whole matter is becoming clearer to me by the moment.'

The Ripper Revealed

Lieutenant Sterling and Professor Peaslee sit across the table from a shackled Persephone Blackstone. The lovely redhead sits demurely sipping a cocktail of bovine blood plasma and wine. She looks around at the iron covered walls and its single heavy door and feels a familiar trapped feeling. The portly professor sitting across from her breaks the spell of melancholy with a genuine wide smile.

'Miss Blackstone, you have my heartfelt condolences. I have performed some tests on your blood and must confess to a certain excitement at the results. It would appear from the data that you are quite dead; yet, here we sit enjoying a pleasant conversation; or so I hope.'

'Thank you, sir for your fair wishes. I am aware of my condition and you must appreciate it to some greater degree as you have provided me with this lovely vintage of wine. I am no monster; what I do I do to survive. The men I take deserve to die; scoundrels all. The one love of my brief life put me in this hellish predicament and I will feel no guilt over his death or any other man's.'

'I apologize for my rudeness, I am Professor Peaslee. I believe you have met Lieutenant Sterling. I want to understand something of what has befallen you, but, I will understand if you do not want to talk about it, just now. Would you tell me how this happened to you, child?'

Persephone looks at the man's kindly face and his genuine interest and decides he is better than the men she has known. He is no Doctor Freiherr to experiment with others against their will or sentence them to a cruel half life. She glances shyly at the young man beside him; Lieutenant Sterling. She waits for the young man to speak or give her some sign of what he is thinking, but, he sits there unconsciously flexing strange metal fingers of his left hand. Somehow, the oversized arm beneath his jacket and its strange silver metal hand takes her thoughts back to Doctor Freiherr's laboratory, the dreadful mansion and the night she gained her freedom from him and started another life. Slowly, Persephone nods to the plump Professor Peaslee, 'It began the night Doctor Freiherr ... I suppose resurrected me would be the right term. I do not know how, only that I was dead and he brought me back to this semblance of life. I believe that because I found the man who murdered me, but, that came later.'

At first, her words come out slowly and hesitantly, as if remembering the events of the past is somehow painful. The two men sit silently, nodding in understanding and encouragement as Persephone relates the horrible

events after her rebirth at Doctor Freiherr's hands.
Lieutenant Sterling's face tightens as she recalls the brutish
Mr. Wilx with his silver collar. Then, she watches the
clouds leave his face revealing a beaming smile when she
tells of Colonel Jones' death and her flight from the
mansion to freedom.

Persephone's speech grows more rapid as she tells
of her flight thru the dark woods only to collapse in a
neglected, deserted shack near sunrise. She tells a lonely
tale of running by moonlight and never tiring. Then, the
lethargy and sluggish feeling that warns her of the coming
dawn. Professor Peaslee scribbles his notes only
interrupting to glean some hint as to a direction taken or
landmarks she may have observed. The young Sterling sits
quietly, absently fingering his holster; in anger at her or the
half remembered circumstances not of her choosing; she
cannot tell which the target of his brooding anger. All at
once, her voice becomes husky and her words turn cold and
sharp.

'I came home to the village to find it oddly dull and
smaller than I remembered it. Maybe it was a trick of the
night, or the fact that I entered familiar grounds in a most
unsavory block of town. I walked along the stones past the
village taverns and the loose women cavorting inside and

outside. The street, while known to me seemed darker, seedier than I remembered it. I steadfastly ignored all the comings and goings on, intent on going home to my parents. I was accosted in a most ungentlemanly fashion, grabbed as it were on my well flank or hind quarters will do as well as any description. I spun round to slap whoever had the nerve to touch me so familiarly and there he was. Standing proud and drunk was my Thomas, smiling from ear to ear. Instead of slapping him, I fell into his arms in relief and welcome. Oh, my Thomas, he was a handsome young man. He cooed sweet words in my ear, but, when I made to step back; he at once became angry. Either because of the liquor or some change; well the change, I suppose, in me; Thomas did not recognize me in the least. Hearing my name and my voice from my lips; he still did not recognize me. He tried to entice me to enter one of the dismal taverns. Instead of answering or making a move, I asked him if he was not in mourning for a recent loss. He smiled and said Susan is not lost, just not here tonight. I was stunned. I asked more pointedly of Miss Blackstone and he replied that he was not seriously engaged to her even before her untimely death. He dared look at me and denounced that they, we, were ever to be married. It was then that I smiled and decided his future.'

'It was then that I decided to settle my debt with Thomas and quench my growing hunger all at the same time. I led him to a deserted building down the street; one I am ashamed to say he once took me to in happier times. On that occasion, I rebuffed his advances and fled the basement. But, on that night, I led him down the dark stone steps and into the basement. I encouraged his advances, then turned on him and hugged him close to me as his warm blood pulsed and gushed at last feeding me and making me feel warm. That night, I lay in the safety of the basement with my Thomas, faithful at last, beside me.'

'The next night, I made it home at last. I stood in the darkness and watched my mother take the black wreath off the front door and my father as he pulled closed the heavy curtains of the front room's bay window. I knew then that I would never be able to go home to my old life. Instead, I went to the stable and saddled Biscuit; he was after all my horse and father told me to take care of him. Biscuit and I rode away that night never to be seen in the village again.'

'My journey cross the countryside is less memorable. In fact, the only clear memories I have are trading Biscuit for the cost of a night time train to the farthest city I knew of, Boston. I still feel bad about leaving him behind, but, what chance would I have to properly care for a horse? Of my time in Boston, you know something of my past actions; but, nothing of the loneliness and need that drove me to them.'

Young Reginald Sterling sits in speechless wonder at the horror and sadness of the young lady's tale. He knows what she is and what she has done; yet, he knows this is not the woman she would have become had things gone differently for her. He sees another life ruined by Doctor Freiherr's evil. Sterling's voice is husky and his throat constrained as he thanks her for her tale, as a host would thank a guest who had read an exceptional poem or told an entertaining story. He shoves his brass clockwork left arm down and thrusts himself out of his wide, overstuffed chair and leaves the windowless cell without a backward glance.

'Do not think him rude, my dear. I am afraid our Mr. Sterling holds a special hatred for this Doctor Freiherr; he almost killed Sterling and his best friend not too long ago. Also, the young man has a big heart and I fear your predicament has saddened him and given him another reason to hate this mad scientist fellow.' So saying, Professor Peaslee stands and begins to walk absently away before remembering his 'guest'. "Oh, my dear, if you would not mind, I am going to go over my notes of your fantastic story and will be just over there if you need anything. For now, I would suggest you try to rest and we will talk again.'

A Gilded Cage

Persephone awakes the next night to find she is still locked safely away in her windowless iron cell. Gone are the bracelets of her shackles. She looks around in wonder; spotting an ornately carved mahogany dressing table that has been brought in and arises with a start when she realizes she is lying on a large goose down bed. She feels a smile beginning to form as she takes in the low table with its tea set and the overstuffed chair with a copy of the Boston style newspaper sitting on it. She starts to laugh as she turns her head and sees an embroidered burgundy dress hanging on a dressing manikin in the corner of the room. The professor's doings or maybe Sterling; whichever one it was they have provided her creature comforts that she has missed so much. Unlike her cell in Colonel Jones' mansion, this one feels warm and safe instead of cold and barren.

Outside Persephone's cell in his cluttered office, Professor Peaslee consults his notes taken while the young lady told her strange tale and begins to perceive a pattern to her movements. He crosses his office and tacks a large map of the New England states on the wall. The scientist mutters to himself and makes calculations of distance using his slide rule. He marks the map with what he believes to be the townships the young vampiress would have passed through on her way to Boston. Slowly, working late into the early morning, he plots her strange journey back to its unholy beginning. The portly man takes off his wire rimmed reading glasses and cleans them while looking at the map covering his wall. The train robberies reported near West Berlin begin to take on a new significance as he looks at Persephone's trail of tears.

The Lair Revealed

Mr. Sterling walks jauntily beside the ever present Sergeant Fitzpatrick as they go to see the Superintendent of the Bureau of Military Information's Boston's office. The young man bows slightly and smiles at Millicent, no longer simply Miss Sumner, as they pass. Warmth wells up in him when she smiles and winks in reply.

Fitzpatrick and Sterling enter their superior's dark wood office and are gripped by a feeling of seriousness and solemn occasion. Both men are surprised to see a smiling Professor Peaslee in his white lab coat; looking totally out of place next to the gray suited serious looking Superintendent.

Professor Peaslee waits for the pleasantries to be over before unrolling his map on the carpeted hardwood floor and without a word sits down beside it. He points with a long wooden dowel to Blackstone Canal and then to Blackstone Village. He moves the dowel to trace Worcester County and points rapidly to the approximate locations of the train robberies leading up to the failed attempt outside Salem.

'I do believe, gentlemen, that I can hazard a fairly accurate conjecture on the whereabouts of Miss

Blackstone's recent captivity and the home of one Colonel Jones, retired.'

The three men turn and stare attentively at the professor each eagerly waiting for the pronouncement. All too soon, they realize the answer will not be so forthcoming. With a collective sigh, the men move to the edges of the map and sit down uncomfortably on the carpet.

'Now, these are the approximate locations of the train robberies that generated so many rumors and stories of iron men and monsters. This is the train station where Miss Blackstone was forced to part with her horse and road the rails to Boston. Here north of Blackstone village, east of the train robberies and west of Miss Blackstone's train lies West Berlin train station. I believe there is a small hamlet nearby that holds the answer to our mystery of the iron men, Colonel Jones and the nefarious Doctor Freiherr' says Professor Peaslee in a calm, warm voice.

'Colonel Jones lives in West Berlin? But, professor, Persephone, that is, Miss Blackstone described a country manor and its grounds; not to mention the large woods surrounding it. How could that be and the mansion be located near a rail station?'

'Precisely, dear boy, it could not. I believe I said the small town near the railroad station to be the clue to finding the mansion of Colonel Jones. He most certainly lives past any town or railroad line, but, no doubt such a man will be known to his neighbors.'

'Well done, Professor. Lieutenant Sterling, Sergeant Fitzpatrick what do you say? What is to be our next step?' says Superintendent Howe while tipping himself to one side and climbing back up to his feet.

'It is certainly the best lead, the only lead that we have' says Sterling.

'Easy enough to prove or disprove; that's for sure. We ride into this hamlet and ask about we are sure to find out if someone there recognizes the colonel's name' says Fitzpatrick.

'Gentlemen, perhaps you are forgetting the tales that were spread after the robberies. That there are such things as Iron Men, we all know to be true. The same can now be said of vampires; or such as appear to be vampires to the uneducated. Perhaps this male vampire raider is also a creature such as Miss Persephone and not the imaginings that we first thought. I would caution against anyone waltzing up to the colonel's front door and inviting themselves in without being prepared for more bizarre and dangerous encounters' says Professor Peaslee.

'A very good observation, professor. Perhaps it is time to borrow a maneuver from our New York District and send a squadron of uniformed troopers led by a Bureau Operative to this train station to run this fox to ground.'

'Begging your pardon, Superintendent. I volunteer to lead the squadron and the search for the mansion.' Sterling stands twisting and turning to relieve the tension he is just now feeling.

'Admirable, young man, but, you are only on loan to us while you recuperate and grow into your new prosthetic. I admit you have been of great service and the professor has almost agreed to release you from his care; but, this should be led by an operative that knows the countryside.'

'In that case, your lordship, I volunteer to lead the soldiers and Lieutenant Sterling can lead the operation while I provide information on the land and he handles the tactics.'

'Hmmph. It does seem inevitable that you two will have yourselves involved in this. If I refuse, next, you two will volunteer to take a temporary reduction in rank so you can be in the squadron; no doubt. So be it, you two know more about the overall situation and perhaps you are just the hounds to lead the pack on this occasion.'

Coffee is soon ordered in and later a light lunch as the men stay in the office and use the professor's map to plan out their route of attack. They debate what troops to take and how many, the Superintendent wisely giving over the duty of picking the troops to Sergeant Fitzpatrick. Professor Peaslee argues for a plan to capture the mansion and all its denizens intact for study. Another debate ensues, but, in the end there is only one choice that will satisfy Sterling and Fitzpatrick. They will apprehend the villainous Doctor Freiherr alive or dead and collect a debt for the victims of the 'The Ripper' and the Iron Men.

At the Station

The cool autumn morning is only hours old as Sergeant Fitzpatrick stands on the stone platform behind the brick single story train station. He smoothes his uniform jacket and looks down at his blue trousers and polished boots; just like the old days of the war, he thinks. Beside him, a young lady in a long burgundy dress smiles, her dark eyes sparkling in the morning as she watches the sergeant fuss with his uniform. She leans forward and gently buttons his collar and adjusts his uniform jacket. 'There, all's right now,' she pronounces. From a nearby wooden bench, the young lady lifts a butcher wrapped package and hands it to Fitzpatrick. He takes the package noticing its heavy weight and eagerly unwraps it to reveal an octagonal barreled rifle with a lever action loop and ornately inscribed brass. The older man leans forward and brushes thick locks of black hair away from her face and kisses her on the cheek.

'This is a fine gift, my darling. You certainly know your way to an old soldier's heart. Many thanks for the grand thought of it,' says the sergeant.

'I want to make sure you come back to me. The gunsmith said this was the best rifle there is. He even threw in a couple boxes of, ah, shells for it.' The young lady notices her face warming in spite of the cool morning air.

'I don't know what I did to prompt such a thoughtful gift, but, I'll be certain to be doing it twice as much when I return.'

The young lady is spared a response as a voice behind her announces the presence of newcomers to the train station.

'Sergeant Fitzpatrick, good morning. I trust we are ready for today's journey?' says Lieutenant Sterling while coming out of the train station's single wooden door.

The sergeant is a little surprised to see Miss Sumner walking behind the lieutenant, but, this does seem to be the place for goodbyes this morning. He holds up his gift and smiles brightly.

'Yes sir, the armored personnel engine is safely loaded and the squad has already boarded and is waiting our pleasure in the Dining Car. Good morning, Miss Sumner. Would ya look at the fine gift my Colleen has given me for our adventure. A brand new Henry Repeating Rifle; fires a heavy .44 caliber shell she does and holds 15 rounds ready to go with just a quick flip of the lever action's handle here. Isn't she a beauty?'

'That she is, sergeant. Now, who might this other beauty I see you with?'

'Oh, I do apologize.' The woman turns around and side steps gracefully to stand beside the sergeant facing the newcomers.

'Colleen O'Connor, sir, miss. Good morning, Mr. Sterling, I would have thought you had seen enough of me at Madame Tussaud's to know me from behind.' Colleen's dark eyes sparkle at the reactions of both Sterling and Miss Sumner.

'Ah, yes. Millicent, Miss O'Connor was at the scene of that murder that the sergeant and I investigated last week. In fact, she introduces us to the establishment's proprietor and was quite ingenious at securing our entrance to the crime scene.'

'Was she now?' Millicent's blue eyes grow icy cold as they take in the long, lustrous black hair flowing down the young lady's back, to the indecently low neckline of the burgundy dress and the high heels of the girl's laced up boots. She hardly has to say a word; Sterling knows there will be more discussion merely by her silence and the glance he receives.

'Are you accompanying the men on whatever it is that is going on here today? Sean wouldn't tell me anything other than he had to be here by nine a.m. to catch the train.' Colleen looks at Millicent's round sun browned face with its small freckles framed by thick flaxen blond hair. The wide yellow gown with its high white lace collar seems a bit staid for a woman not much older than herself.

'No, I came along with Archie after breakfast to see that he made it to the right train station on time. That is we dined together in public this morning and he is not familiar with Charlestown or Boston area in general. Speaking of which, you left this is the carriage.' The lovely blond grins and hands Sterling his kepi.

'Almost lost another hat to those dreaded coachmen! Thank you, Millicent. I am fast wondering how I ever managed without you.' Sterling quickly shoves the baseball cap like kepi on his head and tries to straighten his uniform jacket.

'Sergeant, what say we join the men in the Dining Car.? I do believe it is almost time for the train to depart. Millicent dear, do not look at me like that. I have four hand picked soldiers and the sergeant here to look after me. There is nothing to fear.'

'Actually, Professor Peaslee it was that recommended the men to me. Seems he has had a special squad guarding Miss Blackstone and was eager that they be the ones to accompany us on this journey. Well, Colleen, it's time I was gettin' about my business now that the lieutenant's arrived. I'll call on you when we return; though I don't know how long that will be.'

'Please excuse us ladies and do not worry so. This will be over in no time and we will be back right as rain. Professor Peaslee picked the troopers you say?'

The dark haired beautiful young lady with the blood red dress and its low cut neckline stands quietly beside a more proper looking young lady with golden hair flowing down her yellow gown. The one stands her shoulders drawn forward and her head lowered beside a lady of pride and aristocratic posture. Yet, as the train rumbles away from the station, the longing in their eyes and the look of concern on their faces is identical.

Dining Car

Lieutenant Sterling and the sergeant are just entering the Dining Car when the train pulls away from the station. Sterling reaches out with his metal hand and steadies himself on a nearby chair back; while Fitzpatrick rolls with the motion and walks past him. Down at the far end of the car, four young men in Union blue uniforms stand up and come to attention. None of the men have seen their twenty-first birthday, yet, all have served in the war.

Sterling waits until he is almost at the table with the soldiers before speaking. The young men try not to stare at the spinning gears and metal pistons of Sterling's left arm. For once, he does not notice nor cares about their stares, so intent is he on capturing the doctor and ending the nightmare for himself and Persephone. His right hand adjusts his holstered pistol holding on to it, while the fingers of his left hand begin to flex slowly open and closed.

'Good morning, men. I am Lieutenant Sterling and I believe you all have met Sergeant Fitzpatrick. We have been charged by Superintendent Howe to track down and apprehend, if possible, a war criminal by the name of Doctor Freiherr. It is believed that this man is being given shelter in a country estate somewhere near the town of

Berlin, Massachusetts. We will confirm whether this is indeed so or failing to find said estate; we will follow any clues to the man's whereabouts and run them to ground. As such, I cannot brief you on exactly what this mission will entail or its ultimate destination past the aforementioned town. What I can tell you and what you need to understand is that we believe the doctor to be involved in the train robberies that recently plagued the Bureau and the delivery of the Analytical Engine. Good, I see by your faces that you have some idea of the villains involved in that matter. The doctor is no doubt the least physically dangerous of the men we may well encounter in this pursuit.'

'Beggin' your pardon, sir. If I may clarify the situation for the youngsters, you men have the same responsibility as you always do, Iron Men or no Iron Men. You will follow the lieutenant's orders and clear the way for us to get at this Doctor Freiherr character. The men what staged that train robbery are dead so we know there is no invincibility beneath the iron; just flesh and blood same as any other villain. The lieutenant and I will handle the plannin' and the strategy, our job is to keep you alive to return to your comfortable bunks. Your job is to make sure nothing nasty happens to us while we are doing our job. That's all I have. You have anything to add, lieutenant?'

'No, thank you. Do you men have any questions?'

'Just the one, sir. Will we be marchin' or is there transportation waiting us somewhere along the way? I only ask because we didn't see any horses being loaded at the station.'

'I believe I can best answer that one, soldier. You will all be riding in a steam carriage of my own design. She be an armored personnel engine that will accommodate yourselves and the lieutenant and I' says Fitzpatrick while crossing his arms over his chest and standing even straighter.

'Uh, sergeant. I thought you were bringing the steam carriage onto the train. You brought that iron box on wheels, instead?'

'Oh, not to fret, sir. I made a few modifications after our test outing. I am sure you will approve of how she looks and rides now. Just to ease your mind, I did remove the top so she is open to the air now as you seem to feel a might cramped in her the other day.'

'Well, that is good news I suppose. For now, kindly organize the squad and send someone to find a porter and

have them fetch us some coffee and maybe some loose
meat sandwiches if there are any about.'

Sterling turns and walks back to a wing back chair
and picks up a left over copy of yesterday's newspaper. He
settles into the chair and immediately his eyes are drawn to
an article detailing the Boston Police Department's
announcement of an arrest in the Ripper case. He grins
while reading of Inspector Reid's triumph over the small
band of thugs, two men in particular and a wealthy
merchant's deranged bodyguard now in custody. The train
rumbles past the Back Bay and onto a switch over to a
more south westerly approach to the Central Massachusetts
rail line.

West Berlin Station

The train slows and a blanket of steam rolls out to cover the ground and Sterling gets his first glimpse of the wide, low wooden Victorian train station and its wide wooden planked platform. Sterling stands up amidst the shriek of the train's whistle and the soldiers begin hastily gathering up their gear and weapons. For once, it is Sergeant Fitzpatrick that races down the aisle in a hurry to leave the train and check on his armored steam carriage to determine how it fared in its first train ride.

Sterling waits until the sergeant has passed and is busy navigating the next car before standing up and walking slowly down the aisle; fearing that the iron box on wheels has suffered no damage and come thru its transport without harm. The young operative once more wishes he had taken the initiative to arrange transportation; even a horse saddle would be preferable to the claustrophobic iron coffin on wheels. The soldiers sling their backpacks and file out of the car almost forgotten except for a quick hand signal from the departing lieutenant.

Sterling is facing the four soldiers who stand at attention on the platform. The few passengers from the train are still gathering their luggage and greeting those that came to meet them at the station. The young man notices a passing train conductor and stops him asking a few questions about Colonel Jones' estate and then directions to the town of Berlin. He cringes as he hears the sound of a heavy weight suddenly crashing to the earth followed by the familiar chug and rumbling noise that alerts him that the sergeant's beast has survived. The train conductor's face suddenly pales as the color drains and his mouth opens wide matching his eyes. Sterling turns around fearing some new catastrophe and sees a grinning sergeant Fitzpatrick.

Gone indeed is the iron box's top and the sergeant's head and shoulders are visible behind a heavy half wall of rivets and iron as the armored steam carriage rolls on its four foot high wheels towards the train platform. Sterling notices it is going at a fair clip for such as short distance; then notices all the passengers and train crew are moving calmly, but, steadily away from that end of the platform leaving the four soldiers standing in a line to greet the sergeant. Sterling considers moving, and then decides against it; maybe the steam carriage will crash and he can still hire a wagon and horse team for the rest of the journey. A pall of dust is slung over the edge of the platform and a cloud of black coal smoke and ash floats over the platform causing the soldiers go cough and Sterling to close his eyes.

The Glass Coffin

Sterling opens his eyes waving his kepi in the air in front of him trying to clear it of dust and smoke; revealing a still grinning Fitzpatrick now sitting at a right angle to the platform. Sterling looks on at Sergeant Fitzpatrick standing next to a mast like column in the back of the steam carriage that is covered in rope and a large, heavy tarp. Somehow, the man has turned the beast at the last minute and it is sitting beside the platform perfectly still and aimed at the train station's exit. The sergeant yells to the soldiers as he lowers a hinged panel on the side the of steam carriage revealing a set of ladder like steps built on the inside of the armor plate.

'All aboard, lads!' The sergeant bows to the lieutenant and soon is assisting the stunned soldiers to enter the back compartment of the armored personnel engine. The young men quickly file in and sit down on small cushioned benches built into the walls of the vehicle. Fitzpatrick is still smiling at their shocked expressions when Sterling climbs into the rear compartment and together they pull the heavy panel up and lock it into place.

'Remarkable entrance, sergeant. Quite a change from the last time I had the pleasure of riding in the belly of the beast.' The sergeant leads Sterling to a pair of seats up front bolted to a section of armor dividing the front of the vehicle from the back. Sterling spares a glance back at the soldiers who seem to have all found a place to sit and then to the strange tarp cover and beyond it to the black rectangle that he knows is furnace and boiler for the engine.

'Quite improved. I spoke to a train conductor; he did not know Doctor Freiherr, but, he did give me directions to the town. I shudder to give the order, but, I must. Please take us out of the area and follow that large dirt road over there to your right, if you would please.' Sterling tries to squirm deeper into the bucket seat as the six inch wide iron wheels roll into and out of a large rut in the road and his spine is jarred even before reaching the main section of the dirt road.

'If you do not mind my asking, what is the purpose of the mast and canvas? Surely, we are too heavy for sails to be of any use to us.'

'Not sails. Lads get a move on and remove that tarp for me. Time to unveil the last surprise. Now, lieutenant, before you say anything, just know that I had proper authorization for all the material I used in building this remarkable steam carriage.'

Two of the soldiers gingerly stand up and begin untying the rope and pulling off the heavy tarp covering the mast. Both men quickly sit down as the carriage wheels hit another wide dip in the dirt and from beneath the tarp a shiny brass multiple barreled Gatling Gun swings free. Sterling rights himself in his seat and then turns around to stare down the barrels of the gun.

'What? Where did you get a Gatling Gun? No, I don't want to know. Is that thing safely secured?'

'I had permission to test a new gun that came in to replace one of the turret guns. I'm still working on it. And yes, I am no fool. The Gatling is bolted to the floor. I also liberated a couple of crates of ammunition for the purpose of testing out the new gun.'

'He Seamus, she's wide, heavy and packs a bigger punch than you. Sounds like that barmaid you tried to pickup last weekend.'

'Yeah, Matilda. That was her name.'

'Hey Sergeant. You mind if we name your torture chamber of a steam carriage after the love of Seamus' life.'

'What was that?

'I said you should call this steam carriage Matilda!'

'Matilda, I like it. Thanks, soldier.'

For his part, poor Seamus tries to control the heat rushing to his face, but, does nothing about the murder in his eyes as he sits staring at the soldier's grinning face sitting across from him.

The Road to Nowhere

Fearing how many more hours remain until they reach the town, Sterling wipes the dirt off his face and brushes at his uniform jacket futilely while slowly walking to the back compartment of the armored carrier. He looks out at the column of black smoke trailing behind them and the long dusty trail they are leaving and thinks surprise had better not be a part of Fitzpatrick's attack plan for today. The young former army lieutenant pulls himself upright on the mast of the gun. He smiles at the soldiers as they try to balance themselves on the high back benches and not knock each other off as the vehicle rides the rutted dirt road like an ungainly ship in the ocean riding the waves.

Steadying himself with his left hand, Sterling prepares to try out the crank of the shining brass Gatling gun to make sure no grit has fouled its gears. He is careful to swing the barrels out to the side before cranking the handle and watching the barrels spin round empty. The gun should be empty, but, no sense risking shooting the driver while testing the machine gun.

In truth, though he wouldn't admit it to Fitzpatrick, he is very impressed with the steam snorting beast. The crude heavy rivets and plates of iron add a distinctive personality to the steam carriage that makes its rumbling, growling engine truly at home carrying the soldiers to the battlefield. While having not nearly enough padding or springs on and under the seats for his comfort, the Matilda is a marvelous transport.

Sterling stands like a sailor on watch at the Gatling Gun admiring the countryside and its tall wide evergreen trees. Overhead, the blue sky is broken only by a few white clouds and the low riding sun. The young man braces against the dips and bumps in the road and tries not to notice the soldiers' comments as they fight to stay in their seats. Perhaps standing is a better idea than sitting, after all. He turns his head to avoid a pall of dust thrown up by the front wheels and when he turns back around he notices a slightly narrower dirt road leading off at a right angle from the one they are on.

'Sergeant, I believe our town lies to the right!' he shouts.

'I see it. You best take a seat, I can't promise how that gun's going to handle us turning and you holding onto it for dear life.'

Sterling briskly duck walks up to the front of the steam carriage and braces himself in his seat. As he feared, the sergeant makes no attempt to slow the vehicle down before the wheels turn to the right and the armored beast slides around and leaps onto the new path with a vengeance.

Berlin Massachusetts October 1867

The armored personnel engine, now Matilda, lurches sideways tumbling the soldiers into each other and onto the hard iron floor. The soldiers cough and curse as the coal smoke roars from the smoke stacks at the rear and a cloud of dust covers the vehicle before it rights itself and moves onto the new dirt path. Sterling looks up at a loud shout and the sounds of horses. Heading towards the Matilda on the other side of the path, a horse team and their startled driver stop and stare wide eyed at the curious armored carrier and its dusty passengers. Fitzpatrick tips his hat to the wagon as the Matilda roars past.

'Well, Matilda does make quite a first impression, doesn't she?' says Sterling.

'Stops men dead in their tracks, she does.' Answers Fitzpatrick.

The laughter amongst the soldiers dies quickly at the look from Matilda's almost beau and is quickly replaced by groans as they pick themselves up and try to regain their seats.

The young men look around them at the rows of single story wooden buildings with the wide spaces in between them. Sterling notices a few larger two story buildings breaking the uniform skyline of the main street.

Down the main street rolls the iron steam carriage, drawing curious stares from the townsfolk as it chugs and rumbles past them.

'Sergeant, what say we give the armored personnel engine a rest and take the town on foot? That large clapboard building with the sign 'Bolton Diner' seems a likely spot to start our investigation 'says Sterling.

'Yes, sir. Matilda could use a rest and I'm thinking some water if we can find some. '

Sergeant Fitzpatrick brings the steam carriage to a stop and begins the arcane rituals associated with banking the furnace and venting the steam before he joins the men outside standing on the street. He does not notice their elaborate stretching or the wide grins on their faces at being on solid ground again. On the street, the few people out and about town give the soldiers and the carriage a wide berth as they make their way for home.

'All right, men fall out! Rifles and cartridge boxes only, lads. Leave the rest of your gear stowed. We'll do this exercise in pairs. You two stay with the armored personnel engine while you two come along with the lieutenant and me.'

Sterling is still brushing dust off his uniform jacket when he swaggers into the Bolton Diner and greets the eight or ten people inside with a nod and a smile. Behind him, Fitzpatrick walks in cradling his Henry rifle and quickly steps up beside the lieutenant. Right on his heels, the two young soldiers walk thru the diner's wooden door and fan out left and right. The many small conversations going on in the diner dry up at the sight of the armed invasion.

Sterling takes off his kepi and bangs it against his leg trying to get the road dirt and dust off of his cap. His blue eyes scan the room noticing the simple wooden square tables with their high back chairs. His eyes take in the large square windows in the front and side walls and the doorway in the back wall leading presumably to the kitchen. Of the men, not much stands out; simple folk dressed in rough cotton shirts and heavy wool work trousers. The women are dressed in heavy cotton day dresses made of a more comfortable and practical cut than the hoop skirts worn in Boston and New York. He revises his estimate to a dozen men and women seemingly enjoying their supper before the soldiers' entrance. Already more than a few have noticed the metal patches beneath his uniform sleeve and of course the metal hand is in plain sight.

238 - Charles Reeves

'Help you, gentlemen?' asks a large, balding man as he comes thru the doorway into the diner. Almost as tall as Sterling, he is as wide as Fitzpatrick and while his stained white apron takes some of the punch out of his entrance; the heavy meat cleaver held tight in his fist more than makes up for it. The two young soldiers behind Sterling snap to attention and hold their rifles close in readiness. Sterling smiles as the people in the room instantly relax with the appearance of the familiar man. This surely is Mr. Bolton himself.

'Yes, sir. Glad to make your acquaintance. We have come from the train station and could use a bite to eat and some information' says Sterling holding out his right hand.

Bolton transfers the meat cleaver to a looser grip in his left hand and wipes his hand on his apron before reaching forward and shaking the lieuteant's hand in greeting.

'I'm Joshua Bolton. This is my diner. As for food, we have plenty and good food at that. Now as for information, if you count gossip and mystery, why we got that in good stock as well. But, if you figure to get either with those guns, then we have ourselves a problem.'

'I am Lieutenant Sterling. This is Sergeant Fitzpatrick. We are out from Boston on a, I guess you could say fact finding mission. No threat intended, we can pay for our meals and for the information, if needs be. We are just passing thru town on our way to Colonel Jones' estate.'

'Mary, come out here and assist these gentlemen. Lieutenant, if you want, there's a good table along the far wall that has a good view of the room that should suit you boys just fine. Served with the 28th during the war, myself. Never could eat proper without puttin' my back to a solid wall and sittin' where I could see the rest of the room clearly; especially the doors. You boys just come on in and we'll get you fed right.'

'All right, lads. Let's go get seated and let these nice people get back to their meals.'

The men sit down and are just getting settled in when a girl in a blue dress with a white apron comes up to the table and asks to take their order. The young soldiers look up at the girl's red hair where it spills out from under her bonnet and her clear brown doe eyes above a wide smile; before looking down at the sun browned neck and wide shoulders and sun browned arms. The rest of the girl is hidden beneath the wide apron and blue dress.

'Miss, we'll have four of whatever the daily special is and fresh milk or water, if you please.'

'Young lady, you haven't by any chance heard of a Doctor Freiherr by any chance?'

'The special is loose meat sandwiches. I don't believe I know any Freiherr. Only doctor we have hereabouts is old Doc Parker. That's not who you are looking for is it?'

'No. Actually, our doctor is said to be staying with a Colonel Jones. He may be dead, but, the doctor was supposedly staying at his manor' says Sterling.

'Colonel aint dead sir. Not as I've heard anyway.'

'Oh, yeah. Remember what that girl claimed when she ran in her that first night. Claimed a full grown man, a veteran soldier at that like the colonel was killed in his own house by a young red headed girl. Girl claimed she was some kind of domestic from the colonel's mansion.'

'Mary, I bet he talked to that Constance girl. She said the colonel was dead; then we saw him not a week later walking in the moonlight down Main Street.'

'Oh, yeah. The girl what said she was his maid and then up and ran off with the Thompson's boy.'

'We checked on the colonel a few nights later. There wasn't a scratch on him.'

'Looked better than he has in years, he did.'

'What did this Constance look like, Miss? Did she have red hair and emerald green eyes?' asks Sterling leaning forward in his chair.

'No, she had black hair and mean brown eyes. Girl was touched, she was. Claimed some vampire woman attacked the colonel and killed him and she fled for her life that very night. I never heard such a tale.'

'Now, Mary. How we know she wasn't right about the vampire part? Sure some claim they saw the colonel, but, no one's talked to him in quite a spell. And Constance did disappear.'

'Sam, let's not start that again. Constance and the Thompson boy run off together, that's all.'

'What about my Ruthie? She didn't run off. And Tom Postin and his wife Emily; what happened to them? All of them just disappeared off the face of the earth. And that evil Mr. Wilx coming and going buying up supplies for the manor. He's up to somethin' foul mark my words.'

'Now, Ruthie still might be at her sister's. Tom and Emily Postin, well that one is a mystery. As for Mr. Wilx, he says he is in the colonel's employ and you don't have any reason to disbelieve that. He is a might off putting; I'll give ya that one.'

'Excuse me. What's all this about people disappearing? I do not mean to be indelicate, but, have you checked the woods for bodies? Has anyone spoken to the train station personnel to determine if they have seen these people?' asks Sterling.

'We don't go too far in the woods, these days. Been hearing some strange noises in the woods up towards the Jones estate. And no one at the train station has seen my Ruthie so She ain't at her sister's'

'Sam may be a bit theatrical, but, no one has been seen since they disappeared. I and some others have gone hunting in the woods and I can tell you there is definitely something running loose near the Jones estate. We all heard the shriek and growls of something in the woods. Pat saw something moving from tree to tree, but, couldn't see nothing clearly in the morning fog. We cut short the hunting that day and we don't roam too close to the colonel's land these days.

'So Colonel Jones' estate? How far is it from here and is there a road or trail to it from town?'

'Sure, the old road leads right to it. What, about fifteen miles or there about? You boys just go back out of town same as you came in and then take the fork to the right and it'll take you right to his estate. Don't anyone go out there anymore. Old boy got kinda anti-sociable a while back, but, the road's still there.'

'Thank you, very much. Sergeant, I believe it is time to bring in the other men and give them a chance to break their fast.'

'You two heard the lieutenant. Best be finishing those sandwiches and go relieve your friends so they can grab a bite.'

Sterling finishes his sandwich while watching the soldiers sling their rifles and walk reluctantly out of the diner. This time, the townsfolk hardly look up at the soldiers as they exit. The conversations only grow silent for a moment as two different soldiers walk thru the door and quickly seat themselves at the table. Again, Mary waltzes between the tables with her tray carefully balanced and puts down two plates in front of the young men; before setting a ceramic coffee pot and two cups in front of Sergeant Fitzpatrick and the lieutenant.

'Compliments of my father. Says he never knew an officer that didn't like to finish off a meal with a cup of hot coffee.' The young girl's smile is positively beaming as she spins around and is off again to another table.

'Well, sergeant, what say you? Do we take the road to the estate tonight or wait for day break? The sun is setting for the day and while I dislike traveling in the dark in strange country, I just cannot bring myself to wait until morning knowing we are this close.'

'I'm all for going tonight, myself. We take Matilda and ride straight up to the mansion's front steps and bring your doctor out and head back to good old Boston. We have armor sides and the Gatling Gun for protection; should we run into any Iron Men. With us being seen by so many people today, word of our arrival is bound to reach whoever is hold up at the mansion. Besides, I mounted these chemical lanterns on the front that should provide plenty of light for us. There's no tellin' when I'll get a better chance to test them out.'

'Then it is settled. We finish this excellent coffee, pay up and head for the mansion.'

'You two quit gawking at the ladies and eat up. Time's a wasting and we've miles to go yet.'

The Long, Lonely Road

On the road with fresh directions to the Jones Estate, Lieutenant Sterling mulls over the mystery of the disappearing townspeople. Despite the lack of cushioning, he soon falls into the rhythm of the rolling behemoth and for a while, he is free to just look at the evening sky. Guided by the wide beams of the Matilda's chemical lanterns, he tries to see into the tall evergreen trees lining the dirt trail. Overhead, the moon is on the rise giving some scant light to an otherwise dark countryside. Even the rumble of the engine seems quieter, now that there is no light to see the black smoke and dust trailing behind the steam carriage.

The Matilda chugs along the dirt road with its carbide lanterns lighting the way thru the night. The soldiers settle in and try to ignore the shudders as the heavy iron wheels roll over rocks and branches in the seldom used road. Sterling leans forward over the iron plate trying to see into the gloom of the evergreens lining the room; shadows forming along the edges of the yellow light from the solid fuel as it burns with fizzles and pops. The young man grabs his hat and hastily sits back in his seat as one of the lanterns suddenly flares up brightly. The iron steam carriage is perhaps twelve miles from town when the first sign of trouble is heard. A drop in the boiler's steam pressure is felt as a lurch goes thru the steam carriage and its speed drops off.

Sergeant Fitzpatrick orders one of the soldiers to throw more coal from the shuttle into the furnace. The fire bursts into life, but, the steam pressure falls lower yet. It is only when the sergeant takes out a small lantern and begins to examine his gauges and scratch his head that he realizes they never filled the water tank while they were in the town. The steam pressure is falling and the water supply is about gone. As if in answer to his fears, the Matilda squeals and slows down to a crawl.

Sergeant Fitzpatrick closes valves and puts the steering in neutral while he walks to the rear compartment and examines the boiler. There is no doubt the water level in the boiler is dangerously low. All the men can clearly hear his curses. But, they do not realize the reason for the colorful language or the danger that sits behind them.

'That's it boys, everyone out now! Lieutenant, throw yourself over the side! The boiler water's too low and I don't know if she'll hold!'

The grizzled sergeant turns his head aside and throws open the furnace door then throws a nearby bucket of sand into the furnace to bank the coals. He doesn't bother to close the furnace door, but, simply drops the sand bucket and runs to the side of the armored steam carriage and leaps over the side past the soldiers still climbing down the steps.

Sterling stands up brushing off his uniform while walking over to the soldiers who are all standing in the dark dirt road looking at Sergeant Fitzpatrick's prone back. The young lieutenant is about to ask the older man if he is injured when a high pitched shriek fills the night air causing everyone to duck down. A portion of the boiler's top explodes into the air driven skyward by a stream of super heated steam. An ear piercing whine like a giant kettle that has been left on the stove too long roars from the rear of the Matilda.

Once, the steam is gone and the shrill whistling has stopped, Sergeant Fitzpatrick stands up and begins dusting off his jacket and slaps his hat against his leg repeatedly. Sterling and the young men stand up and look about them wide eyed; still trying to deduce what happened.

'You boys, all right? I swear it's always the little things that get forgotten. I can't believe I didn't think about it before we left town. I even mentioned it when we first stopped and it's not like we didn't have time to take care of the water while we was there.'

'Sergeant, what are you going on about? What in the blue blazes happened just now?'

'Ah, yeah. You remember, lieutenant, when we first stopped in town I said it would be a good idea to get some water for Matilda? Well, I did. Only we didn't get the water. You all just witnessed what can happen when a boiler goes too low and the fire heats what's left over to the point where the metal heats and becomes weak and out pours the steam. Actually, she held together good. Looks like just some metal off the top. I can repair that damage.'

'Ah, sergeant. What about tonight? I am guessing we are not going to ride the rest of the way to Colonel Jones' estate in that.'

'Ah, no sir. From here on out looks like we'll be walking.'

The smiles on the men's faces can be seen even by moonlight. No doubt after the rough ride they've endured none of them are too put out by the prospect of walking. Even lieutenant Sterling can not find a compulsive argument against abandoning the stricken Matilda and taking off on foot for the last portion of the journey.

'All right, men. You heard the Sergeant. Everyone grab your gear and rifle. You, Private, move out to the left and keep an eye out. You, move off to the right and watch for anything moving. We can not be that far from the estate.'

'I don't believe the cursed luck. There is no way that should have happened! Sorry, lieutenant, but, I should have built in a bigger water tank or a spare or something. She'll not roll another step until I repair the boiler, clean out the furnace and I have no idea where the water's going to come from.'

'Leave that for later, Sergeant. None of that is going to happen tonight. Besides, think of it this way, we will arrive much quieter on foot and maintain the element of surprise.'

'Well, there's the silver lining for you, sir. All right lads pick 'em up and put 'em down. We're in the infantry again.'

The small group of soldiers marches down the lonely dirt road their eyes constantly shifting from the emptiness of the trail to the trees and the shadows. Sergeant Fitzpatrick hefts his new Henry rifle and marches with the steady, easy gait of a veteran soldier who has walked many miles over the years. Lieutenant Sterling darts forward to stand at the center of the road with a soldier on each side eager to see what lies ahead. Behind them all, the last two soldiers march slowly watching those ahead of them and watching for anything behind them. Overhead, the moon floats high above the clouds bathing the road in its eerie light.

The Woods Dark and Deep

No one sees the pasty face teenage boy as he speeds from behind a tree and charges the out of the woods towards the foremost soldier on the right. The pale boy slams into the young soldier knocking him down onto the dirt. The soldier pushes his arms out trying to hold back the maniacal youth; astonished by the attack and the strength of the boy. It is while holding him at bay by sheer will that the soldier notices the gummy, glazed eyes and stench of dead flesh coming from his assailant. Without hesitation, the soldier marching behind him rushes forward and kicks the boy off of the soldier. As the boy stands up, snarling with a feral hunger, the second soldier raises his rifle to his shoulder and shoots. The night is pierced by the explosion of black powder as flame leaps from the rifled black powder rifle. The boy falls backward as the bullet explodes into his chest in a bloom of dark blood.

The first soldier gets to his feet and recovers his rifle as the second soldier grounds the butt of his rifle and begins to reload. Both are caught by surprise as the boy pushes himself off the ground and slowly stands up.

Lieutenant Sterling comes out of his shock at the sight of the initial attack and watches horrified as the boy stands back up; a dirt matted blood stained hole in his chest. He draws his pistol and cocks the hammer as he raises the pistol and aims it out in front of him. The boy has just enough time to thrust his arms out in front of him before the pistol fires in a blast of flame and black smoke. The boy's forehead explodes and he falls back to the ground. He doesn't get back up.

Sterling looks at the two soldiers and then at Sergeant Fitzpatrick. The sergeant shrugs his shoulders, but, says nothing. The soldiers move on up the road past the boy's body. Everyone is watching the woods and all more cautiously.

Sterling watches horrified as a pasty faced young woman rushes from deep in the forest and tears at the back of the soldier on his left. The zombie woman's jaws open wide and click shut, but no voice comes forth. The young soldier spins around and steps away from the young woman. She rushes fearlessly forward with her arms flailing trying to grab hold of him. In desperation the soldier uses the butt of his rifle to cave the thing's skull in and she falls to the ground in convulsions. This time it is Sergeant Fitzpatrick who fires, shooting the woman in the head and ending her thrashing about.

'What in the seven gates of Hell is going on out here? Who was that woman and that boy? How can anyone stand back up after taking a shot to the chest like that?'

'Sir, what's going on? They both ran out of opposite sides of the woods, but, weren't no coordinated attack. And, I didn't see a weapon one on either of them.'

'Lieutenant, I think you should have a look at this. This woman is dead.'

'Yes, I should hope so after a rifle shot to the head.'

'Not what I meant, sir. I mean she was dead before I shot her. Look at her eyes and her skin. She's rotting away and that don't happen to freshly killed persons. I should know, I saw enough corpses during the war. This was a corpse walking; if such a thing is possible.'

'Sergeant, I hate to agree with you, but, I see your point. She has obviously started to rot, but, we all saw her run like the wind not a minute ago.'

'What can make a dead thing run? Why'd she attack us anyway?'

'Soldier, I am sure I do not know. Nothing I know of can explain this blasphemous behavior in the dead. I daresay I cannot even credit the mad doctor Freiherr with such an abomination as raising the dead' says Sterling. Then, he cocks his head to the side and starts to think about

Miss Blackstone and begins to realize the true horror of the dead woman on the ground in front of him.

The teenager, Constance, now a shambling undead version of her former self, shuffles thru the underbrush towards the soldiers. The men turn at the rustling noise, but, are unprepared for the sight of the young former maidservant that comes running out of the woods. The men can see the gleam of steel as her tiny hands wave back and forth in front of her. Her skin hangs slackly from her face and already her eyes have turned the color of milk, hiding the brown behind a dull white covering. The nearest soldier turns towards this new threat, but, he is too slow.

Constance's arms, bone white where they show thru her torn blouse move with a strength she never possessed in life as they rake her blade covered hands across the soldier's chest ripping him open. The girl makes no sound as she swings her arms forward; her naked pale forearms marred by crude iron patches that look to have been riveted on along with crude sharply pointed 'knives' of iron sticking out of her fingers. The wounded soldier steps back, but, isn't fast enough to avoid being hit in the side by the girl's right arm. His arm is cut shallowly by her blades and his ribs cry out in protest. He turns to the side and tries to defend himself as she punches with her right arm. He avoids the deadly fist with its iron blades and uses his rifle butt first to knock the girl away from him. He turns to Sterling to say something as the girl regains her feet and shuffles forward. He falls to the ground without a word. Behind him, Constance clacks the steel blades together and shuffles forward.

The young soldiers have all stepped back, surprised by the ferocity of this latest attacker and it is Sterling that comes rushing in at the girl; knocking her to the ground in a tackle. He quickly rolls away as flashing blades bite the air around him.

Sterling lays flat on his back looking up at the zombie's iron laced arms and its hands deformed by the addition of a series of surgically implanted knife blades. He looks at her lifeless cold brown eyes and at her expressionless young face. He briefly wonders who she was before some form of madness turned her into a killing animal. Why, he wonders, would anyone go through the trouble of dressing such a vile creature in a maid's outfit? Without another thought he pushes himself to his knees and throws his left arm forward. Blood erupts from the zombie's face as Sterling's metal fist punches her in the nose flattening it and driving bone into brain. A second punch and the square fingers have crushed the front of the dead girl's skull. The poor teenager falls back onto the road and lies still in death; freed from whatever vile process Doctor Freiherr used on her. Sterling stands up and brushes off the dirt and tries to clean his hand by wiping it furiously on his trouser leg before looking over at the other men.

     'Here's your pistol, sir. You must have dropped it.'

     'Lieutenant, I don't mind the rescue. We were all caught a bit flat footed there, but, I do not want to explain your loss to the Superintendent or Miss Sumner.'

     'Yes, sergeant. I see your point. Of course, the beauty of the dilemma is that I shan't have to face Miss Sumner myself should I make a fatal mistake. The soldier that was felled by whatever horror that was, how bad are his injuries?'

     'He is dead sir. Looks like she cut him deep in the chest. The life poured out of him before he hit the ground.' It is about that time when Sterling realizes they have found the missing townsfolk. The soldiers grumble, but, in the end everyone agrees that the soldier's body will have to stay on the side of the road for now. Time is against them and there is no telling how many more undead townsfolk are roaming the woods waiting to come out.

The End of the Road

The three young soldiers walk cautiously along the dirt road beneath a baleful moon. All three hold their rifles at the ready, bayonets fixed and steady. The three walk abreast along the road. One watches the dark elms and oaks to the left; one watches the dark woods to the right and one walks down the center of the road anxiously eyeing his friends and the empty road ahead. Behind this short skirmish line, Sterling and Fitzpatrick hold their weapons at the ready and watch the young soldiers in front of them; anxious that they should lose no more men to the horrors of the woods.

A garden, once fine, now overgrown with weeds comes into view with a high granite wall behind it. Above the wall, the men can see the slate shingles and twin chimneys of a large mansion. In the center of the high granite wall looms a large archway open with no gate to bar their passage. Black smoke rises from the chimneys to become lost in the night breeze. They have at last reached Colonel Jones' estate.

'Sergeant, hold fast a moment. We have to gather our wits. The original plan had us riding the armored personnel engine into the estate safe behind its armor plate and ready at the Gatling Gun. That is no longer possible and I fear walking boldly down the road and thru the archway is not a prudent course of attack.'

'Yes, sir, I'll be the first to agree it isn't the best plan of action. Though, I'm not much of a mind for going thru the cover of the woods to get close to the entrance; given what we've seen is all ready lurking there in the darkness.'

The two stop and stand in the road discussing the best route to the interior of the granite wall and are soon joined by two of the soldiers. The third has spotted movement within the dark woods to his left and walks steadily onward watching the small movements of low tree branches and the low sounds of twigs snapping beneath something's feet. So intent is he on his unseen quarry that he fails to notice how far ahead of the rest of the troopers he has gotten himself.

'James, get yourself back her man! On the double!' The soldier turns at the sound of his name, but, it is too late. A moment's diversion is all the lurker in the woods has been waiting for and all he needs.

The stable boy's clothes are more rags than proper covering as he runs from between two large trees into the road. James takes on step backwards and swings the butt of his rifle round to crash into the dead boy's cheek sending him spinning to the cold ground. The soldier, now certain what made the noises in the woods, stabs the boy's cold heart with the cold iron of the bayonet. Suddenly, the soldier stands bolt upright as two arms covered by a dirty brown suit coat envelope him and hands made over with cold iron blades plunge deep into his chest.

Sterling looks up as a soldier shouts and sees that one of his charges has gotten far ahead of the group. The lieutenant watches the boy charge from the woods and then is horrified to see a middle aged man in an ill fitting brown suit rush the soldier from behind coming from the woods on the opposite side of the road. He knows the poor young man's fate even before he sees the gleam of metal on the dead thing's hands and watches it plunge those dirty blades deep into the soldier's heart. He aims his pistol, but, it is too late. He fires only after the zombie gentleman has thrown open its arms and turned from the soldier now falling to the ground to lie beside the boy.

Fitzpatrick curses freely as the soldier falls to the ground. The veteran sergeant quickly brings his rifle to his shoulder and sights in the abomination now walking calmly towards the remaining living. A flash of fire beside him and Sterling's pistol explodes punching the zombie in the shoulder. He fires his rifle and smiles as the brown suited man staggers and his chest blooms with black blood. The smile vanishes as the corpse takes another step forward and the boy stands up shuffling forward as well. Fitzpatrick hears the sound of the clinking, clacking of their blades loud in his ears.

The two remaining soldiers both fire their rifles and two more holes are punched in the man's tattered coat. Sterling steadies his pistol and aims at the man still calmly walking towards them as if on his way to church. He can see the dirt and twigs on the man's coat and matted in his brown hair. He can see the iris behind its milky covering. He is struck by the thought that somehow this man climbed out of some shallow grave in the woods just to kill them tonight. He shakes his head to break the spell and pulls the pistol's trigger back aiming just between the cataract marked eyes and pulls gently back on the trigger. The man's head rocks back as the \bullet penetrates its brain and explodes out the back. The brown suited corpse falls.

Fitzpatrick fires two quick rounds into the boy's head and breathes a sigh as the head explodes. The small lifeless body clacks its blades once before falling limply to the ground. The sergeant looks around him at the two soldiers finishing reloading their rifles and at Sterling busily reloading his pistol. Obviously, no one considers the night's evil deeds are done. Surprise gone and cover none existent, the sergeant cocks his rifle and raises it in one arm over his head then thrusts the arm out in front of him.

'Charge, men! Get into that archway before more of the demons come running!'

So saying the middle aged Fitzpatrick takes off at a run for the archway with Sterling running beside him. They take maybe a dozen strides before the two younger soldiers have caught up and threaten to pass them. All four men say nothing as they run the race for their lives past the evil silent trees and into the open mansion grounds.

The Courtyard

Lieutenant Sterling holds his pistol at the ready as he bursts thru the archway onto the cobblestones of the dark courtyard. He barely notices the soldier charge thru the archway with his bayonet thrust forward. Anxiously, Sterling scans the courtyard for signs of life before stopping and staring at the mansion and its heavy oak door. He stands looking at the cheery light spilling out between the heavy curtains of the windows and wonders briefly if they have indeed come to correct mansion. Surely, he thinks, Doctor Freiherr's lair should be a creaking battered sinister looking place instead of this well made brick mansion with its wide stairs and column bedecked porch.

Unseen, Colonel Jones walks silently out of the dark barn. He glides silently over the cobblestones as he slinks along the inside of the granite wall to suddenly grab the soldier from behind. The vampire grins widely and sinks his fangs into the soldier's neck. The soldier lets out a small sigh as the life drains out of him. The clatter of the rifle as it hits the cobblestones is the only warning that Sterling has that something is amiss.

Angrily, the colonel throws the dead soldier to the ground. Sterling turns and shoots the colonel in the chest. The colonel sees the hole explode in his chest and laughs. The old cavalry smiles and advances, drawing his cavalry saber.

Sergeant Fitzpatrick stops in the archway alerted by the pistol shot. He stares unbelieving as an elder gentleman draws his saber and raises it high above his head. A quick glance at Sterling's disbelieving face and Fitzpatrick knows the source of the pistol shot and its target. He raises his rifle to his shoulder and fires.

Colonel Jones feels his body moved as the heavy forty four caliber Henry rifle bullet smashes into his ribs and rips thru him to fly out the other side and into the granite wall beyond. The vampire feels the rage overcome him and rushes towards the interloper. The younger Sterling forgotten for the moment. He soars forward and swings the heavy cavalry saber down towards Fitzpatrick's head.

Fitzpatrick turns the blade aside with the barrel of his rifle wincing at the scar he knows will be left by the steel blade. He quickly twists the rifle and hits Colonel Jones in the face with the rifle butt turning the man's head rapidly and forcefully aside.

Colonel Jones whips the saber back at Fitzpatrick recovering almost instantly from the rifle butt's punishment. Again, the sergeant turns the blade at the cost of his new rifle's shiny barrel. Colonel Jones works the wide saber into a frenzy trying to batter his way past Fitzpatrick's defenses; putting horrible scratches on the brand new Henry rifle's barrel and creating sparks with every swing of his blade. For his part, Fitzpatrick knows he can't hold the saber at bay much longer; his arms growing heavy and the rifle moving farther out of his control with every impact. The sergeant is forced to take a step backwards as the vampire colonel hits his rifle with an especially powerful swing. Madness lights the vampire's eyes and a tiring Fitzpatrick becomes lost in the pearl white fangs that dominate its evil grinning face.

Sterling sees the older man locked in combat with Fitzpatrick and knows the two are too close for a pistol shot. He realizes Fitzpatrick hasn't much time before the saber will win thru his defenses. Without another thought for his pistol or his safety, Sterling charges towards the embattled pair.

Sterling crashes into the vampire like a freight train that has left its tracks. The pair stumble past the surprised Fitzpatrick. Colonel Jones crashes into the stone wall cushioning Sterling. Violently, the vampire spins around throwing Sterling off his back. He raises his saber high and brings it down in a swift slash. And stands mute in shock as Sterling grabs hold of his right hand stopping its swing. The colonel's blood shot eyes grow wide at the sight of the gleaming metal hand holding his immobile. Then, pain as Sterling closes his left hand driven by clockwork gears and unfeeling springs; crushing the bones in the colonel's right hand and slowly bending the metal of the saber's hilt beneath the unfeeling pressure. The vampire punches Sterling and the young lieutenant rocks backwards the air knocked out of him. Holding his ruined right hand against his side, the vampire advances. Sterling blinks rapidly to clear the tears of pain from his eyes and pistons out his left arm. The blind punch spears the vampire's face. The square fingers and silver backed metal hand crash into the vampire's mouth breaking teeth and fang alike. The jaws try to hold the metal mouthful, but, fail breaking with an audible snap.

At the first touch of the hated silver, the vampire screams out in pain; only to be silenced in a flurry of blood and broken teeth. He drops the saber and sags to his knees.

Sterling leaves the colonel rolling on the cobblestones in blood still hurting from the silver's sting and rushes to catch Fitzpatrick before he falls from exhaustion. Sterling slowly helps his friend to the mansion's steps and sits him down. He checks the sergeant for wounds, but, finds only a few shallow cuts from the saber.

Colonel Jones feels the bones in his hand knitting themselves slowly back together and while his jaw is dislocated; the intense icy cold needles from the silver are gone. He watches the young man with the metal arm and hateful silver hand walk up the steps to the mansion's entrance. The hated older man, a sergeant by his stripes, sits quietly on the stairs leaning on his shiny repeating rifle and trying to catch his breath. His mind filled with unfamiliar pain, the colonel rages. He picks up the saber in his left hand and stands up intent on killing the invaders. He scrapes the saber on the cobblestone as he glides slowly towards Sergeant Fitzpatrick.

Sterling and Fitzpatrick both throw themselves flat at the sound of the rifle's blast behind them. Sterling rolls across the front porch and turns kneeling pointing his pistol back at the courtyard. Fitzpatrick squirms on the rough brick steps to look back at the courtyard in surprise. Both men open their mouth in wonder to see a much closer Colonel Jones pitch forward onto the ground. The vampire rolls on the courtyard ground screaming and tearing at his chest with both hands.

The Glass Coffin

Colonel Jones feels the rifle bullet's impact on his back and is shocked at the pain. He feels more shock at the intense fire of the icy cold needles as the silver bullet shatters upon hitting his ribs and tiny slivers of silver pierce his heart; exploding it. He listens to the unfamiliar voice screaming without quite realizing that it is his own voice piercing the night. He claws at his chest, but, cannot remove the bullet or stop the burning icy cold pain. He looks up and sees that the older soldier has come down off the steps and picked up the colonel's saber. The vampire smiles thru shattered teeth. It is truly a relief when Sergeant Fitzpatrick swings the sharp blade and cuts his head from his shoulders.

Sterling kneels on the front porch of the mansion and looks around the courtyard and to the surviving soldier, only to see him calmly reloading his rifle. The young soldier looks at the stunned expression on older men's faces and explains, 'Silver bullet courtesy of Professor Peaslee; can't imagine why, but, he told us it has some unique properties against Miss Blackstone and he thought it might come in handy should we run into any trouble while we was with you. I didn't understand what he meant at the time and it took me a while to remember I still had the bullet.'

Fitzpatrick thanks the young man before ordering him to stand guard on the front porch while they go inside. Sterling shakes his head and slowly opens the mansion's front door; silently vowing to have a long talk with the professor later. He steps into the brightly lit foyer with its oriental carpeting and paneled walls. He looks around at the sliding doors and open sitting room before spying a stairway leading down. He remembers Miss Blackstone's horrifying escape and smiles. Down it is, he thinks.

Sterling walks as quietly as he can down the staircase wondering what fresh horrors await him inside. He thumbs back the trigger of his pistol and has just stepped off the last stair when a meaty fist with hairy knuckles fills his vision. He can almost hear his nose breaking before he lands on his back; the pistol firing into the ceiling.

Mr. Wilx wastes no time in turning and running down the hallway to the laboratory. Throwing open its heavy door he shouts for the doctor to leave thru the secret door. The faithful servant; however cannot resist stopping and picking up a forgotten carpet bag.

'Surrender now or die!' says Sterling in a hoarse voice. He tries to hold the pistol steady while warm blood runs out his nose and into his mouth. He turns his head slightly and spits the blood out.

Wilx uses that brief moment, pulling a short barreled pistol from his waist and firing wildly at his assailant. Sterling ducks by instinct as the bullet impacts somewhere in the hallway. His returning pistol shot exploding a beaker of green fluid which pours over a small gas flame. The liquid burst into flames. Another beaker on the table heats up in the flames and explodes rapidly moving the flames to another beaker and another explosion of chemicals. Wilx turns around to see the secret door standing open and the doctor no where in sight. He sidesteps trying to get away from the heat of the fire just as Sergeant Fitzpatrick fires two quick shots from his Henry repeating rifle striking the glass coffin and causing its pool of fluids to flood outwards causing a massive explosion as they reach the flames. Wilx screams. His coat soaked in chemicals and rapidly engulfed by flames; his flesh torn by shards of glass exploding from the large glass coffin. He sinks to his knees in pain as the room fills with flames. Already the heat forces Sterling back out of the room. He and Fitzpatrick flee to the stairwell as a series of explosions begin to bring down the roof of the doomed laboratory.

In the distance on a dark hilltop, Doctor Freiherr watches the flames engulfing Colonel Jones' estate. The doctor shakes his head at the loss and waste; more for his laboratory and the faithful manservant Mr. Wilx than for the colonel or his home. The colonel, he thinks, served his purpose in furthering his research. He will miss his equipment and the precious chemicals, but, Mr. Wilx's warning has given him his life and freedom. The doctor pats his saddle bag behind him, causing the gold coins inside to clink together. Without another thought for how badly things turned out for others, he turns his horse away from the estate and gallops down the hill, back out of sight.

The Glass Coffin

A Permanent Posting

Sergeant Fitzpatrick and Lieutenant Sterling sit in comfortable high wing backed chairs in a sparsely furnished dark mahogany paneled office on the fourth floor of the Bureau's Boston headquarters. The office door opens and two men feel their bruises and cuts opening as they stand at the Superintendent's unannounced entrance. The stout gentleman walks quietly past them and pours himself a drink before setting into another comfortable chair and lighting a cigar. He looks around at the ornately carved liquor cabinet and the roll top desk with its high backed chair and the oriental carpet covering the room's hardwood floor. Absently, he throws his spent match into the nearby wood fireplace before looking at the room's other occupants. The Superintendent looks at Sergeant Fitzpatrick's bruised smiling face and crudely bandaged burned arm to Lieutenant Sterling's youthful grin on his own battered and bruised face; now given more character by a recently broken nose and smiles ruefully. 'A job well done, both of you.' He declares. 'I have taken the liberty of telegraphing New York of your success in dissuading both the plans of the infamous doctor and the brigands that cost us so dearly when they attempted to abscond with the Analytical Engine and the other train robberies that so plagued our good countryside. I have recommended that Lieutenant Sterling's temporary assignment to Boston be made permanent. That is, if you have no objections, sergeant? I would not want to place too much of an imposition on you asking you to continue as Lieutenant Sterling's aide.'

'I can honestly say that my time at the Bureau and I daresay Boston itself would be a quite a sight duller without the good lieutenant around, sir. I should be most pleased to continue as aide de camp to Lieutenant Sterling' says Fitzpatrick around a wide grin.

'Superintendent, I thank you for the posting and have found the sergeant's advice and company to be most rewarding during my time here. I do not know what I should have done without him.' Sterling says solemnly.

'That is good new gentlemen, seeing as how the orders have already been drawn up. For my part, I dare say the two of you make a fine pair. Judging from the long meeting I had with the Boston Police Department's Superintendent and the Mayor, it is also a certainty the local constabulary may never be the same again.' The Superintendent's face breaks out into a rare smile and he offers both men a cigar. All three men sit enjoying the smooth tobacco and the warmth of the room

'This office was to be Lieutenant Farringdale's. Unfortunately, we have lost contact with him since his telegraph stating that he was coming to Boston on the night train. I am officially assigning this room to the two of you. See that you do not treat it as you have so badly treated the other Bureau property that we have entrusted you with.'

'Oh, almost forgot. Lieutenant Sterling, I believe Miss Sumner is waiting for you outside; seems she has intentions of conducting her own interview as regards your recent adventure. You are dismissed; I would hate to see the young lady grow cross on my account. You are dismissed also, Sergeant Fitzpatrick. Now, both of you go and behave yourself as gentlemen; or as close to as you can manage.'

The two men reply in unison, 'Thank you. Yes, sir.' With that, they turn about and head for the office door; anxious to be on their way. The two men congratulate each other in the hallway before Sterling makes a hasty rush for the stair and Miss Sumner. Sergeant Fitzpatrick watches the younger man running down the hallway and smiles. Straightening his coat and pushes his hat firmly on his head, the sergeant thinks about Madame Tussaud's and a certain brunette with a knack for gift giving and walks slowly towards the stairway.

A Nightmare Ends

On his way down the stairs, Sterling exits suddenly on the second floor and rushes into Professor Peaslee's laboratory. The young man walks slowly and purposely to the entrance to Miss Persephone Blackstone's cell. He nods to the guard standing outside the heavy iron door and asks him to open it. Sterling walks inside the cell and stands beside the wide bed watching a sleeping Persephone. Carefully, he places a note beside the bed on the nightstand and whispers to the sleeping woman, 'Pleasant dreams, dear one. The nightmare is over and the monster is dead.' He brushes the sleeping lady's long, red hair then turns and exits the cell. Back in the laboratory, he nods to the guard and heads for the door. Waiting until the young man is gone, Professor Peaslee walks to the cell and enters quietly, irrationally fearing to wake up the vampires who looks so like she is merely sleeping. Professor Peaslee bends over the coffee table and reads the recently deposited letter.

'My dear Miss Blackstone, while I can do nothing for the suffering you have had to endure, I have at last avenged us both. Doctor Freiherr lies dead, his laboratory consumed by fire. The mansion where you were so cruelly imprisoned is now a pile of rubble and ash. I pray that this fact brings you some comfort. Trust the good Professor

Peaslee, he is a remarkable man and no more warm hearted or honest physician/engineer will ever be found. So, may your dreams be untroubled and may the nightmares end for both of us.'

At sundown, Persephone rises to see the note lying on the table beside a goblet of wine and bovine blood. She sits still as death while she reads and then smiles a wide, toothy smile of genuine warmth and enjoyment. Professor Peaslee stops in front of the cell and for once, she greets him happily and asks where Lieutenant Sterling might be and what remarkable events have taken place while she slept. For his part, the stout hearted professor is more than willing to sit and tell her all that he has heard. Persephone sits near the cell's door talking to the plump professor and slowly realizing that her life has once more changed; quite possibly for the better.

Lovers Reunited

Miss Sumner sits in her horse and carriage and greets the emerging Sterling with a worried look. Mr. Sterling smiles at her solemn face and waves his right arm happily. All the while he is bounding down the huge Victorian mansion's front steps two at a time in a most undignified fashion. The soldiers nearby shake their head ruefully at the uncouth display; until they look over at the object of the young man's haste. Then, they nod their heads and throw a salute to the lucky lieutenant and the lovely Miss Sumner, as Sterling hurriedly, makes his way across the manicured lawn to her horse and carriage.

Sterling remembers to put on his hat, a battered kepi from his days in the US Army, before climbing carefully into the carriage and sitting beside the wistful blonde.

'Hello, Millicent. You needn't look so worried; it really isn't as bad as it looks.'

'I sincerely hope not, Archie dear. I would hate to waste this afternoon on a trip to the hospital. I see you have found a hat that you can keep up with; though I can't say it goes well with your suit and waistcoat.'

'It's like me, my dearest. Not stylish, but, very dependable.'

'Well, I can't say I know you well enough to comment on the dependable portion; I will heartily agree that even dressed up the stylish part is still in doubt.'

'Now, I say. Don't say that; this suit cost me a bundle. I bought it just so I could come out here bandaged and bruised to be properly attired to be abused by your ladyship.' Neither one can help but break into laughter. He because he is in the company of a most desirable woman; she because the man she is starting to care about has come home safely.

Her voice becomes serious as she announces, 'Now, if you don't mind, I thought we would take a stroll around the Commons and then we have been invited to dinner with my parents at their house in Beacon Hill. My parents want to meet a real live hero.'

Sterling's mind begins to reel and his thoughts run wild. Meeting her parents at their home on Beacon Hill? Her parents and presumably the lovely young Millicent as well live in a mansion in the exclusive Beacon Hill neighborhood? Sterling wipes the sweat from his brow despite the cool air; he is suddenly aware that he is pursuing, not just an attractive beautiful, confident lady, but a member of Boston's Brahmin class of elite families. Sterling tries to straighten his coat and loosen his now constricting shirt collar. This dinner the Sumner's family mansion looks more dangerous to the young bachelor than did his assault on Colonel Jones' estate. Beside him, Millicent, her blonde curls escaping from under her hat, sits calmly smiling looking at him. She snaps the reins and the horse team takes off. Sterling looks over as her hair flies in the breeze. He ponders her sun browned face with its small freckles and the deep blue eyes full of promise and kindliness. The young man briefly considers a transfer to London; it would be good to see Reggie... No, he thinks, Boston is his home now. His left hand stops opening and closing, clanking softly beside him and he reaches over to take the reins from his love. If he is to go to his judgment, he is going to drive there himself and not be driven like a sheep to the slaughter. He feels an unfamiliar weight as Millicent leans over and lays her head briefly on his shoulder. Without words, both know his decision is made; and she knows what he is capable of once he makes up his mind.

For it is a time of steam carriages racing beside horse drawn carts along cobblestone streets. It is a time of coal burning furnaces and people working and playing beneath the gaslight. Gone are the gentlemen farmers that founded the American Colonies; this is the time of wealthy bankers and businessmen. It is a time of steam driven horseless carriages and mighty coal gas filled airships sailing high above the countryside. It is a time of grand adventures.

'…it is their duty … to provide new guards for their future security.' – Declaration of Independence

THE END

Partial Timeline:

1842 April – The Honorable Reginald Sterling is born

1850s – New England states excel at Industrialization spurred by designs from England's industrial leaders.

1861-1865 – The War Between the States causes cotton shortage in the northern United States and in England. The blockade of the Confederacy gives rise to Blockade Runners

1861 – Gatling Gun machine gun invented

1861 – Union Balloon Corps founded

1862 – Ironclad steam ships take to the troubled waters. Monitor vs. Merrimac makes naval history

The Glass Coffin

1864 – Aeronautic Division joins the 1st Corps of the Army of the Potomac, first use of airships as offensive weapons

1864 – General Ulysses S. Grant lays siege to Petersburg. Union troops dig trench lines and tear up rails around the city to break the supply line to the Confederate Army

1864 – Lieutenant Sterling wounded at train station and falls under Doctor Freiherr's knife

1865 April 8 – Lee Surrenders to Lt. General Ulysses S. Grant at Appomattox, VA

1865 April 15 – Lincoln Assassinated

1865 April 15 – Vice President Andrew Johnson succeeds Lincoln as President of United States

1866 – President Andrew Johnson re-establishes Bureau of Military Information to combat future confederate sympathizer plots of terrorism and to police the Radical Republicans

1866 – Bureau of Military Information Districts established in those states that stayed loyal to the Union during the War Between the States

1866 – Babbage's Difference Engine No. 2 installed at Bureau of Military Information's New York District Headquarters